*The author gratefully acknowledges
Suzanne Weyn
for her help in
preparing this manuscript.*

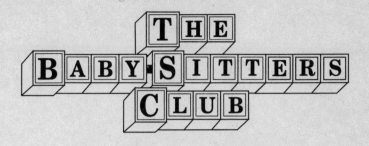

THE BABY-SITTERS CLUB

STACEY'S MOVIE

Ann M. Martin

AN
APPLE
PAPERBACK

SCHOLASTIC INC.
New York Toronto London Auckland Sydney
Mexico City New Delhi Hong Kong

Cover art by Hodges Soileau

No part of this publication may be reproduced in whole or in part, or stored in a retrieval system, or transmitted in any form or by any means, electronic, mechanical, photocopying, recording, or otherwise, without written permission of the publisher. For information regarding permission, write to Scholastic Inc., Attention: Permissions Department, 555 Broadway, New York, NY 10012.

ISBN 0-590-50389-8

12 11 10 9 8 7 6 5 4 3 2 1   9/9 0 1 2 3 4/0

Printed in the U.S.A.   40

First Scholastic printing, May 1999

CHAPTER 1

"Look at the stars arriving in their limos, folks. It's the opening night of the New York Film Festival. Everyone who matters in the film world is here — actors, writers, directors, producers. Here comes this year's hottest new filmmaker (looking gorgeous, I might add). It's the uniquely talented Stacey McGill!"

I tore myself out of the fantasy and glanced at my friend Abby Stevenson. "Here's where the crowd's cheers become so deafening you can no longer hear the announcer," I explained.

Abby wore an amused expression. "Uh . . . Stacey . . . everyone is staring at you," she pointed out.

Glancing around the Stoneybrook Middle School hallway, I saw she was telling the truth. I guess my announcer's voice had been louder than I realized.

Cringing, I covered my red face with my hand. "Oops," I said.

Emily Bernstein had been part of my audience. She's a friend of Abby's and mine. "A little excited about the film class, Stacey?" she asked.

"Just a little," I replied, lowering my hand.

"How could you tell?" asked Abby.

Emily shut her locker. "A wild guess," she said with a laugh. "I signed up for the film class too. I'll see you later." With a wave, she walked down the hall.

I turned back to Abby. "Now that I've made an idiot of myself, let's get to class."

"If you're going to be in film, you have to get used to being in the public eye," said Abby as we started to walk down the hall together.

"But I want to direct," I explained. "I don't want to be a *star*."

"How about a model?" asked Abby.

"Thanks," I replied. "But no." People have told me before that I should think about modeling or acting. I've tried both. Modeling and acting are fun but hard work. And neither one interested me enough to consider as a career.

But I do like to watch movies and figure out how they might have been improved. To be honest, I'm just plain wild about movies in general. I love old movies, new ones, art films, and big blockbuster adventures. I suppose you might say I'm a movie maniac. So I thought I might be able to direct. "Acting seems glamorous, but directing sounds more challenging," I explained.

"If you were a director, you'd still have to appear at movie premieres and do interviews and stuff like that," Abby reminded me.

"True. Though I don't think there will be a lot of media coverage of a film class being offered at a middle school in Stoneybrook, Connecticut." I didn't care, though. Just having a chance to be in this Short Takes class was exciting enough. How many other thirteen-year-olds get to have that experience? Not many.

Short Takes are mini-courses that run for only three weeks at Stoneybrook Middle School, otherwise known as SMS. The subjects are always interesting — Modern Egyptology, Contemporary Political Campaigns, Music Composition, and Architectural Design, to name just a few. Students learn things they couldn't find out about in their regular courses.

This time, not only the programs would be unusual, but the teachers would be too. They were all professionals in their fields. Real composers would teach the music classes. Working archaeologists would talk about Egypt. And the moviemaking class would be taught by Carrie Murphy, a director who's won tons of awards.

Her movies are documentaries, and I really

3

don't follow those. But I knew about her work anyway. We'd received a page of biographies for all the visiting teacher-professionals. Carrie Murphy's bio listed the awards she'd won, including an Academy Award nomination for a short film on Aborigines in the outback of Australia.

I've been fascinated by movies ever since I went to the movies with my parents when I was five and saw a rerelease of Disney's *Cinderella*. And being a New Yorker by birth I've had the chance to see most of the newest movies as soon as they come out since they usually show in Manhattan first.

Not only do they show there, but some are filmed there. Once, when I was eleven, I spent a Saturday afternoon with my friend Laine watching a movie being filmed on a street in downtown Manhattan. (I lived in Manhattan until that year.) Our parents were eating in an outdoor cafe halfway up the block, but Laine and I kept running down the street to watch the movie being filmed.

The street had been blocked off with wooden sawhorses. Big trailers lined both sides of the street, and huge lights on poles had been mounted everywhere.

Laine and I sneaked past the sawhorses and stood between two trailers to watch. It was amazing to see actors I recognized standing around, waiting for their scenes. Some rehearsed their lines. Others talked to the director. Like real people!

Someone turned on a rain machine and the actors walked into the fake rain, getting soaked. The man and woman were supposed to be so in love that they didn't mind walking in the rain.

Laine and I laughed as the water blew our way. But we didn't move from our hiding spot between the trailers. We were too excited to care about getting wet.

Since movies are always being filmed in New York City, our parents took it for granted. But for Laine and me, that day was magical.

That was one of the last exciting things I did with Laine, because not too long after that my family moved here to Stoneybrook. Eventually, Laine and I grew apart, becoming two very different people.

If we were still close, I'd have lots of opportunities to see her. That's because I often go to Manhattan to visit my dad. He and Mom are divorced now. He lives there and she lives here. It's not a super-long train ride, and I enjoy being in the city with him.

I have another reason to love going to the city. My boyfriend, Ethan, lives there. He's sixteen, an art student, completely gorgeous, and totally wonderful.

I met him while I was baby-sitting for some city friends of ours who are artists. Baby-sitting is something I love to do. I even belong to a club called the Baby-sitters Club, or BSC. I'll tell you more about that later since it's a pretty important part of my life.

That Friday, I daydreamed through most of my classes. I imagined making a movie about the life of an art student, starring — Ethan! He'd make a great movie star. I could see myself filming him as he worked, went to class, and studied at museums.

I imagined working day and night without a break to create the finished film.

In reality, I'd have to take breaks to eat from time to time. If I didn't, I'd be imagining myself in the hospital.

I have a condition called diabetes. When you have diabetes, your body can't regulate the amount of sugar in your blood, because it doesn't produce enough of a hormone called insulin. It's serious, but it doesn't have to ruin your life. It definitely doesn't ruin mine. I do have to pay strict attention to what, and when, I eat. No sugary snacks, and I can't let myself get too hungry. I also have to give myself injections of insulin every day.

I'm used to all this by now and it doesn't bother me. But I guess in a more accurate fantasy I'd be working on my film with a plate of carrot and celery sticks by my side. As soon as I'd worked out that hitch, I had no trouble imagining myself at the Academy Awards. *And the winner of the best short-subject documentary is . . . Stacey McGill, for* Portrait of an Art Student.

How cool would that be!? (What would I wear?)

"Earth to Stacey! Come in!"

I turned toward Emily, who had sat down beside me in study hall. We didn't have assigned seats, and I hadn't even realized she was sitting there. "Oh, sorry. I was daydreaming."

"No kidding." She laughed. "I've been trying to get your attention."

"Oh, sorry. Why?"

"I was wondering what your second choice was for a Short Takes class."

"What do you mean?"

"I mean, what will you take if you don't get into moviemaking?"

"Nothing!" I gasped. It hadn't occurred to me that I might not get in. What a horrible idea! I had to take that class.

"We'll get in," I said to Emily. "Don't you think so? I mean, won't we?"

Emily just shrugged.

Well, this was something to worry about. My heart was set on taking that class.

CHAPTER 2

"I know a movie you can make, Stacey," Claudia Kishi suggested that afternoon. She tossed her long, black hair over her shoulders and lifted her hands dramatically as if framing the opening title. *"Attack of the Giant Idiot — The Alan Gray Story."*

I laughed and flopped onto her bed. We were waiting for the other BSC members to arrive for our meeting. "What's the big moron done this time?" I asked.

Alan Gray is what you might call the class clown of the eighth grade, though some of us think of him as the class annoyance.

"Today I had permission to go to the art room during study hall and work on a wood-cut print for a T-shirt," she explained. "I was involved with my print so I barely paid attention to Alan when he came in and left. Then I picked up my T-shirt — and Alan had written across it with permanent marker."

"Oh, no!" I cried. "What did he write?"

" 'I love Alan Gray,' " she reported, rolling her eyes. "As if! He must have done it right there in the room when I wasn't looking. And I wanted to finish it today so I could wear it to the Museum of Modern Art with you tomorrow."

Claudia and I were planning to take the train into Manhattan together and go to the museum with Ethan. Claudia is my best friend, and I like to share my other life with her whenever possible.

"You'll look great, whatever you wear," I assured her. I meant it too. Claudia is the most artistic, original person I've ever met. You can see she's creative just by looking at her, because she puts her personal touch on everything she wears. Today, for instance, she was wearing a tie-dyed T-shirt (which she dyed herself) under a pair of white overall shorts. But these weren't ordinary overalls. She'd painted a rain forest scene over the entire fabric. It made her look like a walking mural. The forest canopy was up by the straps, and mushrooms, rocks, and little lizards sat at the hems.

It doesn't hurt that she's beautiful. Claud is Japanese-American, with flawless skin and a killer smile.

How does she maintain her great skin, shining hair, awesome smile, and normal weight, when she practically lives on a diet of junk food? I have no clue! Somehow she manages, though. Her parents don't approve of the potato chips, popcorn, snack cakes, and candy she loves, so she hides them in her room. Any time you lift a pillow or move a blanket, you're likely to find some cellophane-wrapped treat.

Or you might find a Nancy Drew mystery. Those are Claudia's other secret treats. She keeps them hidden because her parents think she should be reading other, more "intellectual" books.

After thirteen years, Claudia is still a bit of a shock to her parents. Their other daughter, Claudia's sixteen-year-old sister, Janine, is a real-life genius. She's also quiet and studious, like Mr. and Mrs. Kishi. Then there's Claudia, blazing into their lives with her messy creativity, independent spirit, and terrible grades.

Nearly all of Claudia's energy goes to art, with almost none left over for school. She pays only as much attention to it as she's forced to. Her spelling is beyond atrocious. She even had to move back to the seventh grade for awhile, so she could catch up on all the work she daydreamed through the first time around.

But, good grades or not, Claudia is one of a kind and I'm glad she's my best friend.

"Stace, it's almost five-twenty," she said, glancing at her digital clock. "Everyone will be here soon. Let me go down and get your carrot sticks."

"Thanks," I said. Claudia is in charge of hospitality, and she always makes sure there's something I can eat, along with all the junk food.

We meet in her room every Monday, Wednesday, and Friday afternoon from five-thirty until six. Claudia hosts the meetings because she has her own phone number and phone. So when clients call us here to book sitting jobs, they don't tie up her family phone line. There are six of us, so clients can almost always find a sitter.

"Hi, 'bye," Kristy Thomas said to Claudia as they passed in the doorway. (On meeting days, Claud leaves the front door open so we can let ourselves inside.) Abby was with Kristy. They're neighbors, and Kristy's oldest brother, Charlie, often drives them to meetings together.

Kristy slid into Claudia's director's chair, her usual meeting spot. Abby stretched out on the rug, letting her head drop onto her arm. "What are you doing? Yoga?" Kristy asked her.

"Yeah," Abby replied, looking up with a grin. "This position is called the sleeping dog. You do it when you're tired but you still have a sitting job and homework ahead of you."

"In other words, it's a catnap," I commented.

"Exactly."

"Well, wake up," Kristy commanded. It didn't surprise me that Kristy would have no patience for fatigue. I doubt she's ever experienced it. She's a bundle of energy.

Kristy was the one who thought of the club and started it up. She's also the president, the driving force behind everything we do. Whatever she does — whether it's run the BSC, or coach the kids' softball team she started, or spend time with her friends — Kristy throws herself into it one hundred percent.

Kristy is not about appearances. Her style is sporty — mostly jeans, T-shirts, and sneakers. Her long brown hair is usually pulled back in a ponytail. You'd never guess she lives in a mansion in one of Stoneybrook's richest neighborhoods. Her stepdad, Watson Brewer, is a millionaire.

Kristy's not impressed by the mansion. She's just glad it's big enough for all the kids and pets in her family. She has three brothers (two older and one younger), an adopted two-and-a-half-year-old sister, and two younger stepsiblings from Watson's first marriage. Kristy's grandmother also lives with them. Add pets to that and it's one hectic household.

Just two houses down, Abby's home couldn't be more different. Abby's large house (I'm not sure if it counts as a mansion, but it's

12

close) is often empty. That's because her mother, who is an executive at a publishing company in New York, leaves early and comes home late. She's probably the same thing people call my father — a workaholic. That's someone who is overly devoted to his work and puts everything else second. Abby says her mom only became a workaholic after Abby's father died in a car accident back when they lived on Long Island.

Anna, Abby's twin sister, is away from home a lot too. She's very devoted to her violin and is often working with the orchestra at school, taking lessons, or performing. And, when she *is* home, she's busy practicing.

Although Abby and Anna are identical twins, they're not much alike. Not even in looks. They wear their dark, curly hair differently — Anna's is shorter, while Abby's is longer. They both need glasses, but their frames are different. Or one might wear glasses on a day the other is wearing contacts. And while they both have health concerns, the problems are different. Anna wears a brace under her clothing to correct a curved spine, a condition called scoliosis. The brace is hardly noticeable. And after a few years, Anna will be done with it.

Abby has a touch of scoliosis too, though hers isn't severe enough to require a brace.

Abby's health problems are asthma and allergies. She always travels with two inhalers because she never knows when she might need them. Neither problem stops her from being a terrific athlete; she just has to be prepared.

Abby and Anna also have very different energy levels. Anna is serene, able to sit for hours and concentrate on her violin. Sitting still drives Abby crazy. She has to go, go, go. Even her mind can't stop. It's always thinking up jokes and wisecracks. (Although at the moment her go-go energy seemed to be taking a little break.)

"Hi, everybody," Mary Anne Spier said as she entered the room ahead of Claudia, who had returned with my snack. Stepping over Abby, she asked, "What're you doing down there?"

"As my Grandpa Morris would say, my get-up-and-go got up and went," she replied.

Mary Anne stared at her. "Where did it go?"

"I don't know, but if you see it, tell it to come home."

"Okay." Mary Anne didn't press the issue any further. Of all of us, I think Mary Anne might be the one who is best at not expecting life to provide tidy answers to all its questions. Maybe that's because her own life has taken so many twists and turns.

Her mother died when Mary Anne was a

baby. For awhile she lived with her grandparents because her dad, Richard, couldn't cope with single parenting on top of grief. As soon as Richard pulled himself together, he wanted Mary Anne back. Her grandparents didn't want to give her up, but Richard finally convinced them that he'd be a good dad. And he was, although he was pretty strict for a long time. Mary Anne had to battle for every little freedom.

Then one day Mary Anne befriended a new girl in school, Dawn Schafer. Dawn and her brother, Jeff, had moved here with their mother because their parents had recently divorced. Their dad stayed in California, but Mrs. Schafer wanted to return to her hometown, Stoneybrook. Dawn and Mary Anne discovered that their parents had dated in high school. They connived to get them to go out again, and it worked. In fact, it worked so well, they got married. So Dawn and Mary Anne became stepsisters.

They thought this would be wonderful and, mostly, it was. Of course, there were a few feuds and some adjustments to be made along the way, but everybody worked things out. And with Dawn's mom, Sharon, around, Richard loosened up even more.

So, things were great until Dawn decided she missed California and wanted to live there with Jeff (who had already gone back) and her dad. This was a major blow to Mary Anne. Logically she understood that Dawn was doing what was right for her. But emotionally she felt as if Dawn were deserting the family, and Mary Anne in particular. (Despite the initial upset, Dawn and Mary Anne have stayed close and Dawn is an honorary BSC member who comes to meetings when she's in town.)

Luckily for Mary Anne, she had other good friends for support during those tough times. She and Kristy are especially close. When they were younger, people used to think they were sisters, since they are both petite with brown hair and brown eyes. (Now, though, Mary Anne has a more fashionable look and shorter hair.)

Another person who helped a lot is Logan Bruno, Mary Anne's boyfriend. He's a great guy, with sandy blond hair and a soft southern accent. (He's originally from Kentucky.) He's super-involved with sports. He's also an associate member of the BSC. That means he doesn't come to meetings, but we call him if there's a sitting job none of us can cover. He's a terrific sitter.

Our other associate member is Shannon Kilbourne. She lives near Abby and Kristy with her parents and two sisters. For awhile she tried to be a full-time BSC member. Her after-school activities conflicted too often, though, and she had to become an associate again. Shannon also pitches in when we run a fair or have a party or something like that for our kid clients.

Jessi Ramsey flew into the room and checked the clock. It was exactly 5:30. "Whew!" she said, pretending to wipe her brow. Kristy gets annoyed if we're late for meetings, so we all feel the pressure to be on time. "I had a great class today," she said, dropping to the spot on the rug where she usually sits. "But it's almost impossible to make it to Stamford and back in time."

Stamford is the city closest to Stoneybrook. Jessi takes ballet lessons there. She is a talented dancer, and she practically lives for ballet. You can tell just by looking at her. She usually wears her black hair in a bun, ballerina-style. It makes her brown eyes appear huge. And she's so graceful and limber.

The Ramseys live in the house my parents and I lived in when we first moved to Stoney-brook (Mom and Dad were still married then). Jessi's aunt Cecelia lives with them, helping to care for Jessi's younger brother and sister. When the Ramseys, who are African-American, moved in, some of the neighbors weren't particularly glad to see them. Stoneybrook is mostly white, and unfortunately some people here are prejudiced. The Ramseys stood up to them, though, and now they have good friends in Stoneybrook.

"Am I in your way, Jessi?" Abby asked. She was still stretched out on the floor.

"Nope," Jessi replied. "There's extra room here on the rug these days." She didn't say it in a sad or angry way, but I felt bad for her just the same. Recently, her very best friend, Mallory Pike, went off to boarding school in Massachusetts. (She's now also an honorary BSC member.) Like Jessi, Mal is a sixth-grader (the rest of us are in eighth grade) and was a BSC member. They used to sit on the floor, side by side, at every meeting. Jessi is adjusting to Mal's absence, and they've exchanged lots of letters — but it's still hard to lose your best friend.

Jessi is our junior officer. She's junior because, being eleven, she only sits in the afternoons (unless she's watching her own younger sister and brother). That's helpful, though, because it frees the rest of us (who are thirteen) to take evening jobs.

"Any new business?" Kristy began the meeting. Before anyone could speak, the phone rang.

Claudia was in the middle of ripping open a

18

bag of Cheez Doodles, but she was closest to the phone, so she picked it up. "Hello, Baby-sitters Club. Oh, hi, Mrs. Rodowsky. I recognized your voice." She grabbed a long yellow legal pad and began writing down information. "No problem, we'll get right back to you." As Claud was writing, Mary Anne opened the record book on her lap.

Mary Anne is our club secretary, which means she keeps track of all our appointments. She knows everyone's schedules, because they're written in the book. With this information, she can make sure the sitting jobs are assigned fairly and accurately. In all this time, she's never made a scheduling mistake. "What day?" she asked Claudia, who'd hung up.

"Next Friday, right after school," Claudia reported. "Jackie, Archie, and Shea." The Rodowskys are regular clients, so she didn't have to give Mary Anne any more information than that.

Mary Anne checked the book to see who was available. "Abby?" she offered.

Abby waved her away. "Please, no. If anyone else wants the job, take it. It's the one afternoon I'll be free all week and I need a break."

Mary Anne went back to her book. Kristy and I were free, but we were both hoping we'd be involved with the moviemaking Short Takes class. "I'd like to stay free as much as possible that week," I said, "in case we need to do after-school work."

"Me too," Kristy said.

"Okay, that leaves me," Mary Anne informed us. "I'll take it." Claudia nodded and called Mrs. Rodowsky back to tell her to expect Mary Anne.

That's how the club works. Clients call, we assign jobs, then we call the clients back. If we're not busy with phone calls, there's still lots to do. I'm the club treasurer, since I love math. Every Monday, I pass around an envelope and collect dues. (Everyone groans, but they always pay.) We use dues to cover our expenses — reimbursing Claudia for part of her phone bill and paying Charlie to drive Kristy and Abby here. We also use the money to restock our Kid-Kits, cardboard boxes full of fun stuff to take with us on sitting jobs. If there's anything left in the treasury, we might throw a special event for the kids we sit for (a fair, a trip to the mall, something fun like that). Every once in awhile, we treat ourselves to a sleepover or a pizza party.

We also spend meeting time writing in the club notebook, which is like a diary, in which we report about every sitting job we go on. It's a chore, but reading the diary is helpful when you want to catch up on a family you're going to sit for. If there's anything you should know about the kids, it's most likely in the notebook.

Besides a president, a treasurer, a secretary, and a junior officer, we have two more positions I haven't mentioned. Claudia is the vice-president, since we use her room and phone and she's the hospitality pro. Abby is the alternate officer. She knows how to do every job in case someone is absent.

Speaking of Abby, she was still on the floor when the meeting ended that day. As everyone was leaving, I took her aside. "Are you okay?" I asked.

She nodded. "I'm resting so I have the energy to be your agent once you become a big Hollywood director."

"Good," I said with a smile. "Rest fast because the class starts this Monday. And from then on, there will be no stopping me."

I was kidding, of course. But still . . . you never can tell.

CHAPTER 3

"Please, please, please," I murmured Monday morning in homeroom. We were waiting for the Short Takes assignment list to be posted, telling us which class we'd been accepted into.

I met my friends out in the hallway afterward. "I hope I get into Egyptology," Mary Anne said. "But Contemporary Political Campaigns sounds so interesting. I listed it second. I don't really care which one I get."

"We'll find out at lunchtime. I heard that's when the lists will be posted," Kristy said. "If I get my second choice, Business Management, I'll be happy."

I wish I felt as casual about it. But I was set on moviemaking. Maybe it would turn out to be my career.

Alan Gray walked by. "Hello there, girls," he greeted us. "Claudia, why aren't you wearing your T-shirt?"

Claudia glared at him. "Because I used it as a paint rag," she replied.

"Oh, what a shame." He flashed us his most obnoxious grin as he continued down the hall.

"I wonder what Short Takes class he picked?" Abby said. "Introduction to Moronic Behavior?"

"Moronic behavior and Alan need no introduction," Kristy commented. "They're already best friends."

"That's for sure," I agreed. As we headed in our separate directions, I wondered how I'd last until the Short Takes list came out at lunchtime.

"I'm in!" I told my friends happily as I approached the lunch table where we always eat together. "I'm in moviemaking!"

"How do you know?" Mary Anne asked.

"I hung around by the bulletin board until they posted the list," I explained. "You're in too, Kristy."

"All right!" she cried.

Everyone else immediately pushed back their metal chairs, making a horrible clatter. Kristy and I stood alone as they charged out the door to see which classes they'd been assigned.

By the time we'd bought our lunches and returned to the table, they were back, chatting excitedly. It turned out that we'd all been given our first choices. "I can't believe I'll be learning about architectural design from a real architect," said Claudia.

"I think there's a lot of math involved in architecture," I warned her.

"Oh, I don't care. You'll help me." She was so excited that not even math could dampen her enthusiasm. She turned to Mary Anne. "I had an idea for making Egyptian ankh pendants from polymer clay. I'll make you one to wear to your Egyptology class."

"Thanks," Mary Anne replied. "Tombs and mummies are so cool."

"It's a subject you can really get *wrapped up in*," Abby intoned in a horror-movie voice.

"Wrapped up in. Very funny." Kristy snickered. "What are you taking, Abby?"

"Introduction to the Art of Napping," Abby replied.

"You'd better start taking vitamins or something, Abby," Kristy commented.

"Whatever." Despite her joke, Abby looked a little better than she had on Friday. I hoped she'd caught up on her rest over the weekend. "Actually, I'm taking the Athletic Physiology class," she added. "I noticed Jessi is taking the class also. But she takes it at a different time." (Jessi wasn't eating with us because sixth-graders have lunch at a different time too.) "We'll learn all about muscles and how they work when you're moving. It should be cool."

"I can't wait! Ready, set, action!" I cried for no reason other than total excitement.

Carrie Murphy was awesome. She swooped into class in a flowing, black gauze dress that made a perfect backdrop for her exotic, colorful jewelry.

"Hello, everyone," she said, beaming at us. "I am so pleased to be here, excited to be working with tomorrow's award-winning filmmakers."

I loved the way she said that! It didn't sound like a ridiculous fantasy anymore.

"I suppose most of you have read my biography, so you know that documentaries are my speciality. We won't be limited to the documentary form, though. If you have a story to tell, I want you to tell it. Of course, if there is something you want to document, that's fine too. We are completely open in this class." She began handing out some papers. "Before we begin to expand creatively, though, we have just a little paperwork to do."

As we waited for our forms, Kristy leaned over to me. "What's *he* doing here?" she whispered, nodding to Alan.

"Ew. Just ignore him," I whispered back.

Glancing around, I saw that Emily was there, along with Erica Blumberg, her good friend. Pete Black, a nice guy I dated once or twice, sat beside her. Logan was in the class as well, and so was Anna, Abby's twin sister. Also in the class were Sarah Gerstenkorn, Ross Brown, Rick Chow, and Jeff Cummings.

The form Ms. Murphy gave us asked for our name, home phone number, and the kind of video equipment we had available to us. Then there was a space to tell her what aspect of moviemaking most appealed to us.

I filled in the information, saying that I was pretty sure I could use Mom's video camera. Then I wrote, *I'm good with math, so I might want to be a producer since a producer takes care of financial matters. And some of my friends have assumed I'd want to act. But directing is what interests me the most. So that's what I'd like to do in this class.*

There didn't seem to be too much more to say on the subject, so I stood up and put my paper on Ms. Murphy's desk. As I walked back to my desk I noticed Emily scribbling furiously. She'd turned the paper over and was using the back.

How could she think of so much to say?

Then again, she *is* the editor of the school paper, the *SMS Express*, and wants to be a professional journalist. I suppose some people just have a talent for writing.

"Now I'll assign groups," Ms. Murphy announced. Instantly kids started signaling one another, eager to line up groups for themselves.

"Hang on," Ms. Murphy cautioned. *"I'm* making the groups, just putting you together any which way. That's often part of the moviemaking experience. You have to learn to work with people you may never have met before." She selected kids who weren't sitting near one another and put them in three groups of four.

My group consisted of Emily, Erica, Pete, and me. I was pleased.

Kristy landed with Logan and Anna — and Alan! When I looked at her she rolled her eyes at me. Well, at least she was with Logan and Anna. Maybe the three of them could keep Alan under control.

"In the next three weeks you will be working with your groups to create a ten-minute film," Ms. Murphy told us.

"Awesome!"exclaimed Alan.

"One person in each group will be the cinematographer, one will be the screenwriter, one the producer/editor, and one the director," she continued. "I'll give you five minutes to assign yourselves roles."

We pulled our desks into a circle. "Can I direct?" I asked right away. "Did anyone else want that?" They looked at one another and shook their heads. "Great," I said, smiling. "Emily, do you want to be the screenwriter?" I asked.

"Yes," she replied. "Who wants to produce?"

"I do," Pete volunteered.

"That makes me the cinematographer." Erica looked pleased. "That's exactly what I wanted."

When the other groups were ready, Ms. Murphy said, "Now I'm going to shuffle you around. Shake up your worlds."

In our group she made Erica the director, Pete the cinematographer, Emily the producer, and me the screenwriter.

"But why can't we do what we like?" Pete asked.

"Because I want to move you out of your comfort zones," Ms. Murphy replied. "I don't want you to be comfortable; I want you to be challenged. Little sections of your brain that have been asleep will start to wake up."

"But what if I come up with a terrible story?" I asked, worried. "I've never been great at making up stories."

"Filmmaking is a collaborative process. Your group can help you. And you can help the others in their areas. In fact, with that in mind, after I assign you your new roles, I want each group to start brainstorming ideas for your film."

She moved on to the next group. Erica, Emily, Pete, and I stared at one another. Even after all my daydreaming about moviemaking, I was suddenly blank.

"How about something with aliens?" Pete suggested.

"Aliens?" Emily repeated, raising one eyebrow skeptically.

"Why not? All the big movie companies do it."

"That's true," I agreed. "But I can't picture myself writing about aliens. How about something closer to real life?"

"Horror?" Erica suggested.

"That's not exactly real life," Pete scoffed.

"It could be. I guess I mean more like a thriller, really."

"Thrillers usually have lots of action, don't they?" I asked. Everyone nodded. I could picture myself scripting action scenes better than I could envision writing dialogue. "That might work," I said. "It really might."

"What kind of thriller?" Erica asked. Again, we fell silent.

"*Godzilla Comes to Stoneybrook*?" Pete suggested.

"Yeah? And who's going to play Godzilla?" Emily asked.

"We could make special effects," Pete replied.

"What? A plastic T-Rex climbing out of the bathtub and knocking over a Lego village?" Erica laughed.

Pete grinned. "Okay. Maybe not."

"But something like *Terror at SMS* or *The Ghost in Locker One-twelve*," Emily said. "There wouldn't be a lot of special effects. We could have a small cast. And the kids who were in it would think it was fun."

"Sounds good to me," I said. Erica and Pete thought it was a good idea too. So it was settled. I left school that afternoon wondering just how thrilling a story I could write. And feeling very excited about trying.

CHAPTER 4

Over the next few days we learned a lot from Ms. Murphy. First, she played her Oscar-nominated documentary, *Outback Journey*, for us and then we discussed it.

She told how she had gone into the Australian outback and spent time with a group of aboriginal people until they trusted her enough to speak with her on film about their beliefs, customs, and art. We learned how she'd shot tons and tons of film and then cut the film so that only the most interesting parts made it into her documentary. That's the editing process.

She also spoke to us about producing, which involves a lot of things I'd never thought of. Often the producer picks the project. Then he (or she) has to find the money to make the film. Either he provides the money himself or he convinces other people — backers — to put up the funds. The producer may pick the director and have a say in the casting as well as oversee the spending and keep the film within budget.

"When are we going to start?" Jeff Cummings asked. His video camera was on his desk and he was obviously dying to film something.

"Just a few more days," Ms. Murphy assured him. "Your movie will be better if you learn some tricks of the trade before you begin."

Every evening that week I struggled to write my script. For ideas, I rented a whole bunch of thrillers. They often featured a boyfriend-girlfriend team or a brother-sister duo as the stars. And they usually followed a pattern: Everything started out normally, and then slowly things turned stranger and stranger until something horrible was going to happen unless the stars stopped it.

Although I thought of some good ideas, when I sat down at the computer, everything I wrote sounded dumb.

At our Wednesday BSC meeting, I asked Kristy what her group was doing. "We're calling our project *Stoneybrook's Funniest Kids*," she told me. "We'll film the kids we sit for and then just use the parts where they do or say goofy stuff."

"What a great idea," I said. "I bet you thought of it, didn't you?" She grinned proudly in reply. "I knew it," I said. "It's no fair that your group has you — the human Idea Machine. We have no clue what we're doing yet."

That night I watched an old episode of *The Twilight Zone*, and it inspired me. I wrote a script about a geeky, unpopular girl who wishes that everyone would go away and leave her alone. Then she arrives at school one day and finds that everyone *is* gone. She wanders through the school and gets the creepy feeling that something even stranger is going on. Someone writes on the board, even though no one is there. The PA system crackles and she hears singing, but no one is in the office. She smells food cooking in the cafeteria, even though it too is empty. Then, when the final bell rings, all these kids turned zombies burst out of their lockers and chase her around the school!

I thought it had definite possibilities.

"This script is cool," Emily said to me on Thursday morning before class. "Very cool."

I beamed proudly.

"The final scene will require a lot of kids," she mused. "But I bet we can get kids to volunteer. Bursting out of their lockers in gross makeup should be sort of appealing."

"I hope so," I said. "Who do you think should play the girl?"

"How about me? I have a geeky side," Emily said.

"You do not," I protested with an uncomfortable laugh.

"Oh, come on. I'm not saying I *am* a geek, just that I could be believable in the role."

"All right. When you put it that way," I agreed. "We should ask Erica and Pete what they think and then get them to help us recruit kids for the zombie locker scene. Maybe we could start filming on Monday."

"Why wait?" Emily said. "Pete brought his video camera to school today. Let's get as many kids as we can to stay after last period. We can film that scene first and get it out of the way."

"All right," I said. "Let's try."

It was amazingly easy to recruit kids for our big zombie scene. People came up to me all day asking if they could be in the movie. Naturally I said sure. We told kids to show up at my locker after the dismissal bell and to use makeup, paint, or whatever they could think of to look as hideous as possible.

I have to say, SMS students are incredibly creative. You wouldn't believe how awful they looked when they arrived at my locker. Truly gross.

Girls had used eye shadow to create huge dark circles under their eyes and in the hollows of their cheeks. They'd drawn scars across their faces with eyeliner and, naturally, they'd used lipstick to make great-looking blood. A few had emptied their hair gels and sprays — their hair was frozen in some pretty monstrous dos. And some had worked their makeup magic on a handful of the boys who showed up.

Claudia arrived with Jessi and Abby. She'd obviously been in the art room, working. She'd drawn fangs on the other two and spread blue glitter under their eyes. The three of them had wolf noses, and ears sticking up from their hair. Claudia had used huge sheets of white art paper to give them torn paper shirts.

"Do we look horrible, or what?" Abby asked as she spun slowly like a fashion model.

"Perfectly awful," I replied.

Although Claudia, Jessi, and Abby had the best outfits, the other kids had done pretty well. They'd turned their shirts around, twisted them in knots, and taped paper blood onto them. One kid showed up with his pants legs pulled up and rubber snakes wrapped around his legs. (It's amazing the stuff kids bring to school with them on a normal day.)

"All right, everybody!" Erica shouted when the group of about sixteen kids seemed ready. "I've arranged for a bunch of lockers to be left open. Each of you just stand inside a locker and don't mess with anyone's stuff."

At that moment Emily came out of the girls' room. She had fixed her hair in messy braids, had hiked up her jeans above her stomach, and was walking with extremely bad posture. "You're an awesome geek," I complimented her, laughing.

"Why, thank you," she replied.

"Follow me," Erica called to the group. She led us around a corner to where Pete waited, holding his video camera. "Lockers one-fifteen to one-thirty have been left open. Climb into one. When you hear Emily shout, 'Where is everybody?' leap out and chase her down the hall."

"How did Erica manage this?" I asked Emily as "zombies" began climbing into lockers.

"We did it together," she told me. "It wasn't easy. We went to the office and asked for the locker list, then we ran around like crazy finding clusters of kids with adjoining lockers and asking them to leave their doors open for us. We promised to lock them before we leave."

"Amazing," I commented.

"That's the kind of thing producers and directors do," Emily said. She turned to Pete. "Ready?"

He held up his camera. "I hope so. This thing has a ton of switches and buttons on it. I thought it was simpler than this."

Emily, Erica, and I joined him and studied

the camera. It *was* complex-looking. As we tried to figure out what was what, a kid stuck his head out of a locker. "Hey, it's hot in here!"

Another followed. "And cramped. Come on!"

"Just do your best," Erica urged Pete.

"Okay," he agreed anxiously.

"Ready on the set!" Erica shouted. Emily took her place in the middle of the hallway. "Ready, set . . . and action!"

Emily threw her arms wide in frustration. "Where is everybody?!"

Only seven or so kids leaped into the hall, Claudia, Abby, and Jessi among them.

"Cut!" Erica shouted. "What happened?"

She was answered by the rattling of lockers and the sound of muffled shouts. Claudia stepped forward. "Oh, no! They've locked themselves inside."

"Are you kidding?" I cried. Obviously she wasn't. The clatter of lockers was deafening as kids pushed against them from inside. "What are we going to do?" I wailed.

"Don't panic," Emily said, fumbling in her backpack. "I have the master key. The janitor gave it to me, just in case."

Thank goodness she's so organized. Still, it took us close to five minutes to free everybody.

"Next time, don't close the door all the way," Erica instructed the group.

"Next time?" cried one of the girls. "I'm not getting into that locker again. It was too scary. I'm out of here." Two other guys and one more girl left as well. We were down to about twelve monsters.

"Is that enough?" I asked.

My team thought about it, frowning. "I bet I could film them to make it look like more," Pete said. "You know, if I stay ahead of them and sometimes switch to filming only legs and arms."

"It could work," Erica agreed.

"It's not going to be easy to get these kids and these lockers together again. We'd better try to do it now," I added.

"All right, everybody. Take two. Remember not to shut your lockers all the way," called Erica. The remaining kids climbed back inside the lockers, closing them gently. Emily took her position in the hall.

"Where has everybody gone?" she shouted.

Lockers flew open. Kids jumped out.

But, at the same moment, our principal, Mr. Taylor, turned the corner of the hall and walked right into our scene.

You should have seen the look on his face. He leaped back, and even though I was worried we might be in trouble, I had to laugh. He looked so funny.

Emily and Erica raced to him to apologize

and explain what was going on. He took it pretty well but told us we had to be out of there in half an hour so the janitorial staff could clean the floors. We promised we would be.

During take three one girl slipped and another two kids crashed into each other. "We can edit that out," Pete decided, glancing at his watch. "Our time is almost up."

"Thank you all very much for coming," Erica told our actors. "We'll invite you to a screening of your movie debut when we're done."

As the middle school zombies headed down the hall, I turned to my companions. "Why don't we go to my house and see how the film looks," I suggested.

When we reached my house, we settled down in the living room in front of the TV. "I have a copy of one of Ms. Murphy's films," Emily said, taking a videocassette from her backpack. "It's one she hasn't shown us. Do you want to watch it after we see our masterpiece?"

"Yeah," I agreed as I slid our video into the VCR. I hit the play button and eagerly waited for our first bit of film footage.

What I saw was the ceiling of the school. Next there was gray, snowy static. Slowly, though, Emily materialized. She said her line, and the lockers opened.

Much as I hated to admit it, the kids looked totally stupid. They weren't scary at all. Half of them were laughing. Even the makeup I'd thought was so awesome on Claudia, Abby, and Jessi looked amateurish on film. I suppose I'm spoiled by all the fancy makeup and effects I see in movies.

Then, suddenly, there was more video snow and Mr. Taylor's face came on, in close-up. "The janitors will be cleaning the floor in half an hour," he said.

"How did that get there?" Erica cried.

"I don't know," Pete said. "I warned you I wasn't exactly sure how to work the camera."

The film snapped back to our scene, but it just looked ridiculous. We might have been able to pass it off as a spoof, but it wasn't supposed to look as if first-graders had filmed it.

When it was done we eyed one another. "It stinks," Erica said, voicing our thoughts. Everybody nodded.

"What do we do now?" Pete asked glumly.

"For starters, you get someone to show you how to use the camera," Emily said bluntly.

"Well, I didn't *ask* to be the cameraperson, remember?" he shot back defensively. "I was assigned it. I'm doing the best I can."

"I know. Sorry," Emily replied. "It's just not going to be easy to shoot that scene again. And we have to find some better costumes and makeup."

"That's for sure," I agreed unhappily.

Emily put Ms. Murphy's film in the VCR. For a minute I thought she'd made a thriller herself. But it turned out to be a very serious film about girls with eating disorders. She'd interviewed girls who were hospitalized with anorexia, a condition that causes people — primarily girls — to starve themselves because they believe they're too fat.

Our movie seemed dumb by comparison. Maybe it was time to switch gears altogether and take a fresh look at our project.

CHAPTER 5

Friday

Kristy, I understand why you wanted to use the Rodowsky kids in your film. Jackie sure can be funny. Archie is cute too. But I guess being natural doesn't come as, well, naturally to people — even kids — as you'd think.

On Friday after school Mary Anne went directly to the Rodowskys' house for her sitting job. She was looking forward to it because she likes Shea (who's nine), Jackie (who's seven), and Archie (four). The kids are cute and funny.

She was also excited about something out of the ordinary planned for that day: Mr. and Mrs. Rodowsky had given Kristy permission to come and film the boys. Mary Anne figured this was bound to be a riot since the kids — Jackie, in particular — are always doing something entertaining.

Abby once told me that Jackie was trying to hear what she was saying to Shea and he fell through the door he'd been leaning on and into the hallway.

And there was the time Claudia sat for them and the boys tried to paint the backyard shed but wound up painting themselves blue instead and left half the shed unpainted.

On Friday night Mary Anne called me to talk about the filming. No sooner was Mrs. Rodowsky out the door that afternoon than Kristy, Logan, Anna, and Alan arrived. "All right, guys, just act natural," Kristy said to the Rodowsky boys. "Pretend we're not even here."

"How can we do that?" asked Shea, who sat

at a table working on a jigsaw puzzle. Kristy swung the camera at him.

"So, Shea, tell me what's so interesting about puzzles," she said. Mary Anne knew Kristy was hoping for a funny comeback.

Shea looked at her blankly. "I don't know. They're just fun."

Alan tapped Kristy's shoulder. "Uh, Kristy, did you forget? I'm the director. You just work the camera."

"Alan, I know these kids. You don't," she replied as she whirled around and aimed her lens at Jackie, who sat on the couch. "Jackie, why don't you, um, stand up and do something?" she suggested.

"Like what?"

"Well . . ." she considered. "Walk up the stairs."

Archie climbed on the couch beside Jackie and began jumping around and making silly faces. "Look at me, Kristy. I'm doing something."

"Cut it out, Archie," Jackie scolded his little brother.

Kristy kept the camera trained on Jackie. "Jackie, move away from him. Go somewhere else."

"No thanks. I'll stay here," Jackie declined.

Archie stopped jumping and stood on his

head on the couch. "How about this, Kristy? This is a good one."

"I'll get to you in a minute, Archie," Kristy told him.

Alan turned to Anna and Logan, who were standing by the door, watching. "Would you remind her that I'm supposed to decide what we film and how?"

"Kristy," Logan spoke up. "Is there something you'd like Alan, Anna, and me to do?"

"Logan!" Alan cried. "Don't ask her that. You're supposed to ask *me* that."

Logan sighed. "You're not the boss, you're just the director, Alan."

"That makes me the boss," he shot back.

"I thought Anna was the boss. She's the producer," Logan argued.

"I'm not exactly the boss," Anna said. "I'm more the coordinator and money person."

"See? I'm supposed to be boss," Alan insisted.

"Oh, Alan, grow up," Kristy put in. She returned her attention to Jackie. "Jackie, tell us about some of the funny things that have happened to you lately."

Jackie tightened his lips, then stood up and walked stiffly into the kitchen. Mary Anne hurried after him. "What's the matter?" she asked him.

He folded his arms. "Kristy's making fun of me," he said, crossing his arms.

"I don't think so." Mary Anne pulled up a kitchen chair beside him. "She thinks you're naturally funny, and she's making a video about funny kids."

"Oh, yeah? Well, why is she ignoring Archie, then? I think Kristy just wants me to fall or bump into furniture or do something dumb."

Actually, Mary Anne had to admit to herself, he might be right. When nobody else is around, we do refer to Jackie as "the Walking Disaster." Kristy was probably counting on him to live up to his reputation. Mary Anne was surprised that Jackie had picked up on that. "Okay, well . . . you don't have to be in the video if you don't want to be," she said to him gently. "Kristy would never want you to feel bad. She just likes funny kids."

Jackie smiled for the first time that afternoon. "Great!" he exclaimed. "Can I go play in the backyard?"

"Sure."

Mary Anne returned to the living room. Taking Kristy's arm, she drew her aside and told her she'd given Jackie permission not to be in the movie.

"What did you do that for?" Kristy demanded.

"I didn't want him to feel bad."

"Hmm, well, neither do I," Kristy agreed. "Hey, Archie," she called. "Let me see that hula-hoop dance you wanted to show me." Archie launched into a hopping-around dance he seemed to make up as he went along.

Everyone smiled at him — except for Alan, who stood in a corner fuming with his arms folded.

Mary Anne wandered over to the window to check on Jackie. She smiled as she saw him engaged in a make-believe karate battle with an invisible foe. He was in a world all his own.

Kristy moved alongside her and gazed over her shoulder. At that exact moment, Jackie stepped back, and his foot landed in a sand pail. It stuck fast, and he hopped on one foot, desperately trying to kick the pail off the other foot.

"Yes!" Kristy whispered excitedly as she lifted the camera to film him. This was clearly the moment she'd been waiting for.

Yet it seemed so wrong to Mary Anne. Jackie had said he didn't want to be in the movie. He didn't even know he was being filmed. She slid her hand across the camera lens.

"Mary Anne!" Kristy cried. "What are you doing?"

"He doesn't want to be in the movie," Mary Anne reminded her.

"Oh, come on! This is perfect," Kristy

protested. "It's exactly what I'm looking for." She pushed Mary Anne's hand away from the camera. But Jackie had succeeded in removing the pail by then. "You made me miss it," she snapped. Frowning, Kristy turned away from Mary Anne. "Okay, everybody, I think we've gotten all we're going to get here. Let's go."

"Thank you, Ms. Cameraperson, for deciding that for me," Alan complained.

"You're welcome," she replied, heading for the door.

Logan stopped to talk to Mary Anne. "Thanks for letting us film," he said quietly. "I'll call you later."

"Good luck," Mary Anne said to him warily. "Do you think this can possibly work, with Kristy and Alan sniping at each other?"

Logan shrugged. "I don't have much choice. Maybe today was just a bumpy start."

"Maybe," she said, squeezing his hand. "For your sake, I hope it gets smoother."

CHAPTER 6

They say that Einstein's great theory of relativity came to him in a dream. I can't say anything that spectacular occurred to me while dreaming. But here's what did happen.

I went to bed Friday night feeling very uneasy. Was I worried about the movie? That sounded likely, but I felt it might be more than that.

When I finally fell asleep, I had a crazy dream. I was in the outback of Australia. The landscape was dry and covered with scrubby bushes, and somehow I just knew that's where I was. (In dreams you know things like that. Besides, a kangaroo hopped by.) But in the middle of this unfamiliar landscape stood SMS. The entire building was plunked down right there! Ms. Murphy sat cross-legged on the roof. She smiled and waved to me. A bunch of kids ran by the front of the school, laughing. Kristy ran after them with her camera to her eye, trying to film them. And that's when I woke up.

The moon was shining on my face, and for a second I wasn't sure where I was. "Weird dream," I muttered. Then I rolled over and fell asleep again.

But in the morning I woke with a great idea, and I think I can thank the dream for it.

I called Erica, Pete, and Emily. They agreed to come over around lunchtime. When they showed up, we gathered in my living room, and that's when I sprang it on them. "The problem with our movie is that it's dumb," I said.

"What's dumb about it?" Erica protested.

"It's not dumb," Pete objected at the same time. "It's supposed to be fun, and it is."

Emily just sat quietly on the couch wearing a thoughtful expression.

"All right," I continued. "Maybe dumb is the wrong word. What I mean is . . . it's not important. Ms. Murphy is making documentaries about native peoples of Australia and kids with serious eating problems. We're just playing around. Why can't we think of something more meaningful and do a documentary about it?"

"Ms. Murphy didn't say we had to do a documentary," Pete said. "It sounds so boring."

"It doesn't have to be," I argued. "Kristy, Logan, Anna, and Alan are doing one about the funny things kids do."

"What do you want to document?" Erica asked.

I remembered my dream. Now I saw clearly what it meant. SMS is a world unto itself. It has its own culture worth exploring, just like that of the Aborigines. (All right, maybe that was stretching it a bit, but it was the same idea.) "Ourselves," I answered. "We'll explore the culture of kids at SMS."

"I don't get it," Pete said.

Emily sat forward. "We could interview kids at school, our friends," she said, obviously excited by my idea. "It would be so much more meaningful than our thriller — and easier. There would be a lot less to set up."

"I like the easier part," Pete admitted.

"Yeah, easier is good," Erica agreed. "But what would we ask them?"

There was a moment of silence as we thought about this. "How they feel," I said after a moment. "What it's like to be a middle school student."

"Do you think anyone could answer that?" Pete said skeptically. "I'm not sure I could."

Emily stood up. "Let's see if you can," she suggested.

"What do you mean?" Pete asked.

"Stacey, do you have a video camera?" she asked.

I nodded. "And I already have permission to use it." I ran to the front hall and found it on a shelf. It was loaded with a blank cassette.

"Okay, Erica, you're the director," Emily said. "Where do you want Pete to sit?"

She shrugged. "Outside?"

"Okay," she agreed. "Let's go outside." It was a beautiful, warm day. We sat Pete on my front stoop so that the planter of tulips on the steps would show.

"I don't want to sit in a bunch of flowers," Pete objected.

"Oh, I guess that's not manly enough," Emily teased. She suggested he move over by a maple tree. "Is that more masculine?"

He made a face at her but sat in front of the tree.

Switching on the camera, I aimed the lens at Pete. "This is Pete Black," I said. "Pete, what's it like to be a middle school student?"

"I told you, I couldn't answer that," he replied, shrugging.

"Maybe we have to find another way to put it," Erica said.

"Pete, what's the most difficult thing in your life?" Emily asked suddenly.

"Don't you think that's a little personal?" Pete replied.

"If we only ask polite questions, we'll only get polite answers," Emily said. "We need to be personal."

"It seems to me that interviewers on TV — people like Oprah — start out polite and then slowly become more personal," I pointed out.

"All right," Emily said. "Pete, how was your day so far today?"

"The best," Pete replied. "I love doing homework on a gorgeous Saturday."

"Come on, Pete, be serious," Emily scolded him.

"Okay. My day's been interesting so far," Pete said more seriously. "I mean, I didn't expect to be doing this at all. I figured I'd just call some guys and hang out. And then I received this unexpected phone call from Stacey. That's all right, though. I like it when life is surprising. There aren't enough surprises in life."

"Do you think everyone's life is lacking in surprise or just yours?" Emily asked.

"I think when you're older life might become more interesting. Like, say, if I could drive, then maybe I could go somewhere. And, actually, I *can* drive. I know how to. I'm just not *allowed* to. That annoys me, makes me feel stuck."

"Would you say being stuck is the most difficult part of being thirteen?" she questioned.

"You know, it might be. I feel as if I can really handle a lot of things I'm not allowed to do. Like a job. I'm sick of mowing lawns and delivering papers to earn money. I know I could handle a job in the mall, where I'd make better money. I could work a cash register or wait on people. But I can't get a job like that until I'm sixteen. That's not fair. Why can't I take a test to see if I'm qualified? Why does everything have to be based on age?"

"Why do you want to earn so much money?" Erica asked.

"So I can buy a car and go somewhere!" Pete answered with unexpected heat. "And I want to make sure I can go to college when the time comes — because I don't want to be stuck here in Stoneybrook all my life."

"What's wrong with Stoneybrook?" I asked from behind my camera.

"Nothing! I'm just sick of it!" he cried.

"Cut!" Erica shouted.

"That was great!" I said, switching off the camera. "It was interesting, and you got around to some personal stuff."

Pete seemed uneasy. "Did I sound stupid?"

"No way!" Erica insisted. "I bet a lot of kids feel that way. I know I do. It helps to hear someone else talk about the same things you're feeling."

"Really?" he asked.

"Yes!" Emily said. "This is definitely going to work. We can interview our friends, but we should talk to other kids too. Kids who hang out together tend to be alike in a general way. We're going to have to interview kids we don't know as well too, maybe even kids we don't really like."

"Kids we don't like don't like us either," Erica pointed out. "They might not talk to us."

"But we don't all know and like the same kids, so we'll work something out," Emily replied.

"Are we going to keep my interview in the film?" Pete asked.

"Well, I'm the editor," Emily answered. "When I see all the interviews together I'll decide which are the most interesting, revealing ones and then I'll cut out the rest. Do you want to be in it?"

"I'm not sure," he admitted. "Part of me feels strange about it, but now that it's filmed, another part thinks it might be cool to be in a movie."

"We'll probably keep yours," Emily said. "I'm sure it will be one of the best ones."

I was really excited about our idea. I was out of the scriptwriting business. Now I'd be writing questions for us to ask. And it looked as if I'd be conducting interviews too. I was kind of nervous about that. I *knew* Pete — and he'd surprised me with his answers. What other unexpected things was I going to learn about my classmates and friends?

CHAPTER 7

"Thanks for doing this, Abby," I said. It was Monday during lunch. My film crew and I had decided to interview Abby, and she'd agreed.

We wanted her to sit in the field at the side of SMS. We'd film her so that there was mostly blue sky in the background. As director, Erica had decided that would be pretty striking.

"Abby, turn your head more toward the school," Erica directed.

"Why?"

"I just think it will look better that way."

Abby smiled at me. "Oh, these temperamental directors," she joked.

I returned her smile as I sat facing her cross-legged. "And, roll 'em." Erica signaled Pete to start filming. He put the camera to his eye and began moving around us, which was a little distracting. I did my best to ignore him.

As the interviewer, I had decided to use the technique that had worked so well with Pete.

"So, Abby, how has your day been so far?"

"Long!" Abby said. "Extremely long."

"Why is that?"

"Every morning my mother's alarm goes off at five. Five! And it's *so loud.* I can never go back to sleep, but at that hour I can't think clearly enough to do anything very useful. I try to catch up on school reading, since I'm always behind in that. That's not easy because Mom actually starts leaving messages on people's voice mail in the office while she's getting dressed in her bedroom."

She stopped and laughed softly. "Still in her nightgown and she's already bugging people for stuff. So, she's blabbing away, then Anna starts practicing her violin at about six-thirty. It's not easy to read under those conditions."

I smiled at her sympathetically. "Sounds rough."

"I know. Poor me. I don't mean to whine. Maybe it's because soccer season has started, but it all seems like too much."

I tried to think of a probing question, something that would make interesting film footage. "What's your favorite part of the day?" I asked. (Weak, I know.)

"Bedtime!"

That answer kind of cut things dead. I couldn't think of where to go from there. We just sat staring at each other.

"Oh, very funny." Emily broke the silence. "I don't believe it. Bedtime isn't your favorite."

"I suppose not," Abby agreed. "I like soccer. And gym can be fun. BSC meetings are cool. And I like to baby-sit. I don't know. There are so many favorite parts that I can't fit them all into one day. I mean I *can* and I *do*. But it's really a lot sometimes."

"It sounds as though you're like your mother," Emily observed. "Maybe you both like to fill your schedules with more than you can handle."

"No way!" Abby cried. "She's exactly who I don't want to be like."

"She's got too much to do and so do you," Emily went on. "You're going from morning until night, just like she is."

Abby jumped to her feet. "That's not true!" She stopped as a horrified expression swept her face. "Wow! What if it is true? I never thought of it like that. You might be right. But I don't want to live my life like that — always rushed and pressed for time."

She began to wander away from the camera. "Abby, where are you going?" I called after her.

"Sorry, I have to go think about this," she said in a distracted way. "I really can't talk anymore." She continued walking toward the school.

"Cut!" Erica instructed Pete.

I turned to my film crew. "I'm sorry. I didn't think she'd just walk away like that."

"Are you kidding?" Emily said gleefully. "Do you know how great that's going to be on film? We captured a person experiencing a profound revelation. It was . . . real-life drama!"

"Roll 'em!" Erica cried.

It was after school that same day. Pete aimed his camera at Jessi, who was seated under a willow tree near the edge of the school grounds. "How was your day, Jessi?" Emily asked. (She and I had agreed to take turns conducting the interviews.)

"Good, I guess," she answered. She seemed a little nervous and glanced at me. I nodded encouragingly. "I just had regular classes. I don't have ballet class this afternoon, so I have a little time to kill between now and our BSC meeting. Do you want to hear about the BSC?"

"Maybe later," Emily said. "Right now, I'd like to know what you do with the in-between time."

"Well, often I take ballet classes, which I love. Dance is very important to me. I also read. Horse books are my favorite."

"What else do you do in your spare time?" Emily asked.

Jessi shrugged. "Not much. I used to go to

Mallory's house. She's my best friend, even though now she's going to boarding school."

"So, you've recently lost your best friend?" Emily asked.

"Not that recently. A few months ago. I have other friends, but not many who are my own age."

"Or from your own African-American background," Emily added.

I cringed when she said that. It seemed almost rude.

"That's not exactly true," Jessi answered. "I have African-American friends — and some Latina ones too — in New York City. I met them when I was involved in a dance program called Dance New York. I'm still in touch with them. Two of my friends came up for a sleepover not long ago. They got along great with my other friends from Stoneybrook."

"How was that experience for you?" Emily asked.

"Fun," Jessi replied.

"No problems?"

"I don't know. Maybe I sometimes feel as if my Stoneybrook friends will be bored if I go on and on about dance. I think even Mallory was bored when I talked about it too much. But with my dance friends, I can talk forever about the difficulty of performing certain steps and jumps and also the fun of it. It was a little weird being part of two such different groups."

"Is it also easier to be around other kids from similar backgrounds?" Emily asked. I wished she'd stop with that line of questioning.

"Not really," Jessi answered. "Before Stoneybrook, I came from a pretty integrated town in New Jersey. I'm used to being around white kids."

White kids — that sounded so strange coming from Jessi. It never occurred to me that she might think of us as white kids.

"But doesn't it put a strain on you, being a minority here in Stoneybrook?"

"Emily," I cut in. "Do you think this is really — "

"It's okay." Jessi cut me off. She turned back to Emily. "You know, no one has ever asked me that before. But it's true. It can be a strain."

My jaw fell open. I hadn't realized that.

"I feel it more now that Mallory is gone. Before, I was never alone, but without Mallory I am. I'm suddenly more aware that I stand out, that I'm different."

"How does that affect you?" Emily asked.

"I feel that I always have to be on my best behavior. I can never look messy, or act dumb, or goof off on my schoolwork. I feel almost as if I'm representing my race in a white world, and sometimes I resent the pressure."

Boy, was I shocked to hear that.

"And you feel more relaxed with your Dance New York friends?" Emily inquired.

I breathed in deeply, waiting for her to say no.

"Yes. I suppose that I have more in common with them and I don't feel I always have to be perfect."

"Jessi," I cried softly.

It was almost as though she'd forgotten I was there. Once I spoke, she looked slightly panicked. "But my friends here are great," she added. "Really, they're the best."

"But you don't feel totally relaxed with them?" Emily prompted.

"They're older than me," Jessi replied. "That makes a difference. And I suppose being the only African-American in the group does make me feel different sometimes."

I became aware that Pete was now filming me, instead of Jessi. He must have felt that the amazed, distressed expression on my face was as much a part of this interview as Jessi's words.

"What's wrong? I'm not good enough to be in your film?"

That was how Cokie Mason greeted us on Tuesday morning. Emily, Erica, and I were standing at my locker discussing who to interview next.

The last person we'd have thought of was Cokie. Even though she runs with a crowd of kids some might consider popular, none of us particularly likes her or her friends.

But here was the opportunity we'd been waiting for — the chance to interview someone we disliked. The three of us exchanged glances.

"We'll interview you, Cokie," Emily spoke up.

Judging from Cokie's expression, this shocked her. She'd probably been expecting an argument. "Okay," she said in a small voice.

"Meet us outside at lunchtime," Erica told her.

"I'm not skipping lunch," Cokie protested.

Typical Cokie. Even after we agreed to what she wanted, she gave us a hard time. "Then come after you eat," I said.

That afternoon, she showed up fifteen minutes after lunch began. Cokie thought it would be "cool" if she sat on the back end of a car in the parking lot. She then spent almost ten minutes selecting the nicest and cleanest car. Finally, though, she was seated and ready.

"Let's roll." Erica signaled Pete.

"Wait, wait," Cokie said, sliding off the car trunk.

"Cut!" Erica yelled. "What is it?"

"I forgot to fix my makeup." Cokie dug around in her shoulder bag. We sighed and waited for her to touch up her eye shadow, liner, and lipstick in the side mirror of the car.

"You look gorgeous, now come on," Emily prodded her as she fussed with her hair.

"Oh, all right," Cokie replied, climbing back on the car. "You don't understand about looking good, Emily. But it's important to me."

Emily shot me a look that said, *Can you believe her?*

I rolled my eyes in reply.

Once Cokie was seated again, I began. "So how was your morning?"

"Cool," she replied.

"What was cool about it?"

"Everything. I mean . . . not school . . . but the rest of it was cool."

"But all you've done so far is attend school," I pointed out.

"School is just *part* of going to school," she answered in the overly patient voice you'd use to explain something very obvious to a child. "There're things like friends, and clothes, and boys, and all the stuff you do in between classes. That's the real reason you go to school."

"Tell us about boys," Emily jumped in.

"Boys are people who can be jerky but who can also be adorable." Here she shot Pete a flirtatious smile. I couldn't believe it — he smiled back at her.

"Boys are pretty much the most important thing in the life of a middle school girl," she continued confidently. "I, myself, am between boyfriends right now. I don't have to be. But this time I'm holding out for a really good one. I've had it with the losers I've been dating. My next boyfriend will be ultimately cool."

"What would make him ultimately cool?" I asked.

"The same things that make any person ultimately cool. Good looks. Nice clothes. He shouldn't be failing school, but he shouldn't be that excited about it either. You don't want someone who spends his life studying or uses words you have to look up. If he were the captain of a team, that would be all right."

"What about a good sense of humor, integrity, intelligence?" Emily asked.

Cokie gazed at her blankly. "Those are okay, but they don't make you cool."

"Are you for real, Cokie?" I couldn't help

saying. "Do you and your friends really think like that?"

"Like what?"

"Well, are good looks and nice clothes really on the top of your list? You mean you'd never even consider hanging around with someone who didn't have the right clothes or who was plain?"

"You mean someone like you?" she cracked. "Actually, Stacey, you could hang with us if you wanted to. You have the right look. But you would never consider it. You're just as snobby as you think my friends are. You only want to be with your little BSC pals because you think they're so much better than us."

I realized she was right. I did think my friends and I were better than Cokie and her friends.

"Oh, don't look so bent out of shape," she continued. "All groups think they're the best and don't want someone who doesn't fit in. Even the geeks hang out with other geeks. I bet that, secretly, they think being geeky is the only way to be. That's how it is in the world. At least that's how it is in middle school."

It wasn't exactly the most positive thing I'd ever heard. But her theory did have a ring of truth to it.

Who would have guessed that Cokie Mason

would give me something to think about seriously?

Our project was turning out to be surprisingly revealing. But the first two days of filming didn't prepare me for what was to come.

CHAPTER 8

During lunch the next day, we filmed Claudia in the art room. I couldn't think of any place more suitable. "Can you sit by the window?" Pete requested. "There's a lot of light coming in."

"Sure," Claudia agreed with a smile. She seemed perfectly at ease, probably because she was in her most natural environment.

I was proud of myself for thinking of it. Maybe I was getting the hang of this.

Emily's questions still seemed to be producing more interesting responses than mine were, though. Probably because she was less polite, more probing. I decided I'd try to be a more hard-hitting interviewer from now on. After all, I'd been most direct with Cokie and it had produced my most interesting interview so far.

Still, I figured I'd start with the easy opener that had been working so well. "Claudia, how was your day today?"

"Excellent, completely excellent," she replied. "I love Wednesday because I have art in the morning, followed by a study period. Then I ask for a pass to come to the art room, so it's like having a double art period."

"You're such a terrific artist," I said. "Which of the arts do you like best?"

She thought about it. "I can't decide. One month I think I'd like to spend all my time printmaking. Then, the next, I'm totally into fashion design. I hope someday I'll be able to choose one. But for now I'm just having fun."

"Is there anything you like about school besides art?" I asked.

Her brow creased into a frown. "Stacey, you know there isn't," she replied.

"Pretend I'm not me," I whispered quickly, then I returned to my normal voice. "Tell us a little about school."

"I hate it! You know that."

"What do you hate about it?"

She thought a moment. "I hate that it keeps me from doing what I love. I hate that it's so competitive too. You have to do well in middle school so you'll be placed in an honors class in high school, so that you'll get into a good college."

"I suppose that's true," I commented. I hadn't thought of it that way before.

"Of course it is," she said. "If the thing you do well at is art, no one really cares. It's considered this very minor subject compared to English or math. I mean, where is the room for individuality?"

Her voice climbed as she became more caught up in her subject. "There is none. You know, you hear all this talk about how you are the only unique you and everyone has their own special talent. It's what they say, but it's not the way the school operates. What they really mean is, *Do well in math, science, or language and you'll be rewarded. Otherwise, you're a failure.*"

Emily jumped in once again. "But hasn't the artist been misunderstood throughout history?"

"Maybe so, but that doesn't make it right," Claudia answered. "And the school shouldn't try to pretend they respect or reward individuality when they don't. They should just lay it out: *We're going to make your life as difficult as we can.*"

"Do you think it's really that extreme?" I asked. It seemed to me that she was going a bit overboard.

Claudia folded her arms. "Yes. Absolutely."

Wow! Even though Claud is my best friend I hadn't realized what she was up against or

71

how angry it made her. These interviews certainly were an eye-opener for me.

"I don't want to do this," Emily protested after school that day. "I really have to get this edition out." Pete had already started filming her. We were in the *SMS Express* office.

"That's why we're here," I reminded her. "So you can work on the paper and also be involved in the film."

She sat at her desk, a large teacher-sized one crowded with papers. "How was your day today, Emily?" I asked.

"Very interesting. How was yours?"

"Fine. But let's talk about you. Do you like being editor of the paper?"

"Most of the time I love it. Sometimes the deadline pressure is overwhelming. Kids don't turn their articles in on time. Or sometimes they're so badly written I have to redo them. I suppose I like to take charge, though."

"You seem to be able to handle it," I agreed.

"You're a take-charge type too, Stacey, but you don't take charge of anything," she observed. "Why is that?"

"Well, my life is very busy. Also, I'm always traveling back and forth to the city. I don't want to commit to things that might require me to be available on the weekends when I —

hey, wait!" I cried. "I'm interviewing you, re-member?"

"Oh, yeah," she said with a grin. She'd turned the tables on me.

"What's the best part of your day?" I asked.

"English class and working on the paper."

Surprisingly, Emily wasn't easy to interview. I sat for a second, stumped. What should I ask her next? None of the questions I'd prepared seemed right.

"What's the best part for you?" she asked.

"Oh, no you don't," I said.

"It's math, isn't it?" she continued. "I know you love math. But you can't make math a ca-reer."

"Of course you can," I cried. "There's plenty you can do with a college degree in math. There's physics, engineering."

"Who would want to be an engineer?" she scoffed.

"Are you kidding? Engineering is a huge field. You can plan bridges, or you can work on computer things, or you could design house-hold appliances. You might even be involved in the space program or robotics. It's endless."

"Is that what you'd like to do?" she asked.

"I'm not sure," I admitted. "All along I've been thinking I might go into engineering. But now I'm wondering if filmmaking might be fun. It's not a math field, but you do have to know how to budget."

Finally I realized she'd done it again. "Is there some reason you don't want to talk about yourself?" I asked pointedly.

"No, but I'm a writer and a journalist. We're happier observing than being observed."

"You already consider yourself a writer and a journalist even though you're only thirteen?"

"Yes, I do. I'm sure that's what I'll be."

"I wish I felt that certain about the future."

"That's one of the biggest problems I see among middle school kids," she said. "Fear of the future. It's so unknown that it can be terrifying."

"Cut!" Erica cried. "That stuff about the future would be a great way to end the film."

"It would be," Pete agreed. "Even though we found out more about the interviewer than the person being interviewed."

Some daffodils had blossomed near the back entrance of the school. It seemed like a good place to interview Mary Anne at lunchtime on Thursday.

Emily had suggested her, but I wasn't sure she'd give a good interview. I love Mary Anne. She's the best. But sometimes she's so sweet and polite that she doesn't always say what's on her mind because she doesn't want to hurt anyone's feelings. Also, she's more of a listener than a talker. Maybe this was my chance to practice being a more dynamic interviewer. It might take that something extra to get a reaction from Mary Anne.

"How was your day today, Mary Anne?" I asked, once Erica had given me the go-ahead.

"The same as usual," she replied casually.

"How was your Short Takes Egyptology class?"

She shrugged. "To be honest . . . a little boring. I thought I'd learn something more than I already knew. But so far it's been the same information you hear about on public television. I love those shows, but I thought this would tell me more."

"And it hasn't?"

"No. It's been a big fat bore."

I narrowed my eyes. Mary Anne is a pretty even-tempered person, but today she seemed moody for some reason. "Are you okay?" I asked, half forgetting that Pete was filming.

"I'm all right."

I figured everyone is entitled to a bad day. And there was no law that said she had to love her Short Takes class. So I continued. "Mary Anne, your friends know you as a sunny kind of person, someone who looks for the positive side of things. But don't you ever get mad?"

"Of course I do," she said harshly. In fact, it seemed I'd just *made* her mad. But maybe that was good.

"Well, what makes you angry?"

"Lots of things. Like . . . I don't know . . . like people who can't be nice. People who yell. The people at our school who think they're the best — you know who I mean."

She sighed. "I even get mad at teachers because they can be so unfair. Some of them play favorites all the time."

This was unexpectedly great stuff. "Do you get mad at your parents?" I asked.

"Sometimes. I know I shouldn't. Especially with my mother. Sometimes I am *so* mad at her."

"Sharon?" I asked. I thought they had a good relationship.

"Not Sharon," she snapped. *"My mother!* I hate her for not being there. Why did she have to die?"

Mary Anne stopped speaking as a stunned expression came over her face. It was as if she'd surprised even herself with her last statement.

"Can we stop now?" Mary Anne requested in a small voice. Tears had come to her eyes.

"Cut," Erica instructed Pete.

Mary Anne stood up and walked away, wiping her eyes. Emily leaned close and whispered to me, "That was a great interview."

I nodded. It was probably the best one so far.

And from the person I'd expected it from least.

CHAPTER 9

Friday

Kristy, you need to get a grip. you are completely power-mad with your film. you don't seem to care who you make mad or inconvenience. maybe you should go to Hollywood. you're showing all the obnoxious qualities it takes to make it big.

When the Pike family needs the BSC, we always send two sitters, because there are seven kids (not counting Mallory, that is). On Friday afternoon, the two sitters were Abby and Kristy.

But that day Kristy was there in a dual role: baby-sitter and filmmaker.

Abby arrived first and was there to open the door when Kristy arrived with Anna, Logan, and Alan. "Hi, guys," she greeted them. She stifled a smile when she noticed Alan. He was wearing a baseball cap and sunglasses — just to make it absolutely clear that he was the director.

Mrs. Pike came down the stairs as they walked in. She turned toward her children, who were gathered in the living room. "All right, kids, you'd better behave, because Kristy is going to capture your every move on video," she told them with a teasing smile.

"We always behave," said nine-year-old Vanessa, who sat on the couch writing on a pad. Abby was sure she was composing a poem, since that's her favorite pastime.

"Yeah, we're better than good," added Margo, who is seven. "We're excellent." She was sitting at the other end of the couch, where she had been reading a book to Claire, who is five.

"Finish the book," Claire urged her impatiently.

The ten-year-old triplets, Adam, Byron, and Jordan, sat cross-legged on the floor, playing a game. They were too engrossed in the game to respond to their mother's comment.

"Why aren't you guys playing that in the rec room?" Mrs. Pike asked them as their noise level rose.

"Because the light isn't working down there," Adam told her.

Mrs. Pike sighed. "All right. I'll look at it when I get back."

Nicky, who's eight, came in from the kitchen holding his baseball mitt. "Anybody want to play catch?" he asked.

"No thanks," Jordan answered. The rest let his answer stand for them as well.

Mrs. Pike gave Abby the number of the hairdresser where she'd be and left.

"Okay, kids," Kristy jumped right in. "What can you show me?"

"I've written you a poem," Vanessa volunteered.

"Let's have it," Kristy said, aiming her camera at Vanessa.

Alan stepped between Kristy and Vanessa. "Excuse me," he said sharply. "I believe it's my decision whether or not we film a poem."

"You're in my way, Alan," Kristy said calmly as she stepped around him. "Go ahead, Vanessa."

Vanessa stood and held her pad in front of her. "Hey, kids, gather 'round/Kristy's makin' a movie, complete with sound/It's all about kids who are silly/ goofy, loopy, willy-nilly/So if you are feeling nutty/ Call up Kristy—she'll be your buddy."

Kristy put down her camera. "That's excellent, Vanessa. We'll introduce the film with this."

"That will be so cute," Anna agreed.

"Wait a minute!" Alan cried. "Did I say cut? I don't remember saying cut. And we're not starting the film with that poem."

He turned to Vanessa. "No offense, little girl, but this is not Kristy's movie, so we can't use your poem."

Vanessa scowled at him. "Don't call me little girl."

"Don't listen to him," Kristy told her.

Logan stepped into the room from the doorway where he and Anna had been standing with Abby. "Kristy, Alan does have a point. And he *is* the director."

"Hey, look what I can do!" Claire cried out.

Kristy whirled toward her, camera held to her eye.

Claire began to do a somersault on the couch. Abby saw that she was about to veer off of it and onto the coffee table. She tore across the room and caught Claire midtumble.

"Hey, why'd you do that?" Kristy objected.

"Because she was about to bang into the table and hurt herself," Abby replied angrily. "How could you just stand there filming it?"

"She wasn't going to hit the table," Kristy scoffed.

After that, she filmed Vanessa, Margo, and Nicky singing a silly song about a goat who ate everything in sight but saved the day when he coughed up a washline full of clothing he'd swallowed and flagged down a train that was about to crash.

Unfortunately, the performance involved throwing clothing into the air. Abby went around gathering up tossed sneakers, head-bands, and sweaters, while Kristy filmed.

"Look! Film this!" Byron called to her. She turned her camera toward him. He had climbed on Adam's back. Jordan was in the process of climbing on Byron's.

"Not so close to that lamp," Abby said warningly as she eyed the glass light fixture on the table next to them.

"We can't move now," Adam grunted from the bottom of the pile.

"They're fine," Kristy said as she filmed.

Nicky began climbing on top of Jordan while his brothers shouted for him to get down. "I can do it," he insisted. But as he put his knee on Jordan's back, Adam buckled and the whole stack came crashing down — into the table.

Abby lunged for the lamp as it teetered to one side. She caught hold of the shade just as it was about to smash onto the floor.

She turned angrily toward Kristy. "Why don't we play this tape for Mrs. Pike, and show her what a great baby-sitting job you're doing!"

"Oh, chill, Abby," Kristy snapped at her.

"Hey, you guys, don't fight," Margo said.

"Mind your own business, Margo," Abby barked at her.

Margo's jaw dropped and tears welled in her eyes.

"Now look what you've done," Kristy cried.

"I'm sorry, Margo," Abby apologized. "Really. I'm mad at Kristy, not you."

Margo sniffed. "That's okay."

"What are you mad at *me* for?" Kristy asked in disbelief. "I didn't do anything."

"Well, you certainly haven't done any baby-sitting. You've been too busy being a one-woman filmmaking crew."

"I'll say," said Alan.

"Oh, Alan, shut up," Kristy said. "Anyway, we're done for the day."

Alan stared at her. "I didn't say cut."

"Cut!" Kristy shouted.

CHAPTER 10

Later that afternoon, I sat in Claudia's room wishing Pete were there to film the meeting. I thought it would be great if he could capture the tension between Abby and Kristy.

Kristy sat in Claudia's director's chair wearing a frosty expression. Abby slumped on Claudia's bed, looking everywhere but at Kristy.

I could easily imagine the camera moving back and forth between them, capturing their angry expressions and waiting for the spark that would ignite an explosion. It would be fabulous film footage.

When the phone rang, Claudia picked it up. "Baby-sitters Club." She took down some information and hung up. "It was Mrs. Wilder," she told us, "for this Sunday."

Mary Anne opened the record book. As I looked at her I realized she hadn't said a word since she'd arrived. Was she still upset about the interview? Her expression was blank, hard to read.

"Kristy, want the job?" she offered.

"Haven't you heard? Kristy's given up baby-sitting," Abby spoke up. "She's just a filmmaker now."

Kristy glared at her, then turned to Mary Anne. "Yes, I'll take the job. Unlike some people who are too exhausted these days to do more than one thing, *I* am able to baby-sit and deal with the rest of my life. Some of us can walk and chew bubble gum at the same time."

"And film and direct," Abby shot back. "Are you also going to edit the movie?"

"That's Logan's job, but filmmaking is a team effort," Kristy replied sharply. "Maybe if you were in the class you'd have just the slightest idea of what you were talking about."

"Well, unlike you, I don't think I know *everything*."

Luckily, the phone rang again, cutting short the Fight of the Century. It didn't stop ringing until the end of the meeting, leaving no time for further arguing.

At six, Abby stood and picked up the phone. "Hello, Mom? Could you come and get me at Claudia's, please?" she said. "Yes, but I'd rather not ride with them today," she continued. "I'll explain on the way home. Thanks."

"Fine," Kristy grumbled as she left. "Fine with me . . . you big baby."

Since I had a lot of homework, I wanted to get home pretty quickly too. Mary Anne was waiting for me at the bottom of the stairs. "Can we talk?" she asked.

"Sure," I replied.

"I'll walk with you." Mary Anne fell into step beside me as we left Claudia's, but she didn't say anything.

"What did you want to talk about?" I asked.

"Well . . ."

"Well, what?"

"Would it be possible . . . would you mind if . . . ?" Again she hesitated. "I'd like you to cut my interview out of your film," she said at last.

"All of it?" I cried, surprised.

"At least the part about my being mad at my mother," she said. "I don't want that on film."

"What bothers you about it?" I asked.

She shook her head. "I don't want that to be my only public comment about my mother. I don't remember her, but she was still my mother."

"Our film isn't exactly going to play in the mall," I reminded her.

"Yeah, but you never know who will see it. There's another thing too. I don't want Sharon to see it. She tries so hard to be a good stepmother. I wouldn't want her to hear me say that I don't consider her my mother."

"But do you?" I asked.

"She's a kind of mother," Mary Anne replied. "But I don't know if it's the same. I've never had a mother that I remember, so how would I know? Sharon and I had an argument before I saw you. I think that's why I was in such a bad mood."

"What did you argue about?"

"You know how she's so forgetful and scatterbrained? Well, she forgot to pick up a dress of mine from the dry cleaner. She said she would get it. If she hadn't said that, I'd have picked it up myself. I wanted to wear it when I go out with Logan tomorrow. But she just forgot."

"Can't you get it tomorrow morning?" I asked.

"I probably can. But at the time I just felt crabby, because she's always forgetting stuff, and I said so. Then that made her angry and she said I don't appreciate how much she does remember to do for Dad and me. Before I knew it we were fighting. You know how I hate to fight."

"Yeah." Mary Anne would rather die than fight. "So, you were thinking that maybe if your own mother were alive she wouldn't forget things that are important to you?" I guessed.

"Exactly. I know it was stupid, but it's how I felt at the time."

"Everyone gets angry once in awhile," I said.

"Now do you understand why I want that part out of your film?"

"I do, but . . ."

"But what?"

"It's not really up to me to decide," I told her. "We don't operate like Kristy and her group." I grinned. "We've been deciding things together. In fact, Emily was the one who wanted you for our project in the first place."

"Oh, come on, Stacey," she pleaded. "You can do this for me. I know you can."

I probably could. But I wasn't sure I wanted to.

Our film was about life in middle school and Mary Anne had given us a pretty clear picture of hers. Or at least a part of her life.

"I'll discuss it with Emily, Pete, and Erica," I said, being careful not to promise anything.

"Oh, thank you. I am so relieved!"

I wasn't sure she should be.

CHAPTER 11

Pete, Erica, Emily, and I met at Pete's house to review our film the next day, Saturday. It looked good. Pete's camera work had improved tremendously since the beginning of the project.

After several minutes, Mary Anne's face appeared on the screen. As it did, I reached over to the VCR and paused the tape.

"We need to talk about this," I told the others. "Mary Anne is feeling weird about her interview and would like to be cut out."

"No way!" Emily cried.

"But if she doesn't want to be in the film, shouldn't she have some say about that?" I said.

"It's our best interview," Emily pointed out. "It has great emotion. It shows the loneliness a lot of middle school kids feel. What could be more moving? Her mother died when she was just a baby. What's more dramatic than that?"

90

"Besides that, it's technically the best," Pete added. "The sun is hitting her just right and the sound is great."

"Once Mary Anne agreed to be interviewed, she gave up the right to control the result," Emily insisted.

"Says who?" I exclaimed.

"Say the rules of journalism, and they apply to video journalism too. Unless the person asks to speak off the record, it's *on* the record."

I looked at Erica. "What do you think?"

She shook her head. "I can't make up my mind. I don't want Mary Anne to be unhappy, but I don't want to lose our best footage either."

"We're not done," I reminded them. "There will be other good interviews."

"We don't know that," Emily said.

"Emily," I cried. "How can you be so hard on Mary Anne? You wouldn't reveal the littlest thing about yourself when you were interviewed."

"I did so," she protested. "I said I wanted to be a journalist."

"Oh, like that's so personal," I scoffed.

"We're not talking about me. We're discussing our project, and I think the Mary Anne interview should stay."

"Me too," said Pete.

"I guess I do also," Erica agreed.

I sighed. Why couldn't I be more like Kristy and insist on having things my way? Well, that wasn't me and I couldn't. "If that's how you all feel," I muttered.

They said nothing — just looked at me, their expressions apologetic but firm. And, to be honest, the part of me that cared about the film thought it should stay too.

Unfortunately, another part of me was Mary Anne's friend. The filmmaker and the friend were at war right now.

"I'll tell Mary Anne and she'll just have to understand," I said with a sigh.

That afternoon Emily interviewed Erica. "Sure I get mad," she answered when Emily asked her the same question I'd asked Mary Anne. "But everyone gets mad. I'm no different."

"But what things make you mad?" Emily pressed.

"The usual," she replied. "War, violence, pollution."

Watching from the couch, I shook my head in frustration. Like Emily, Erica was not going to reveal much. I wondered if that was because they'd watched too many of the other interviews. Erica probably didn't want to wind up like Mary Anne, having said something she couldn't take back.

"I think that's enough," Erica told Pete after several more unrevealing answers to Emily's questions.

Pete's doorbell rang. "I have a surprise interview subject," he announced, heading for the door.

He returned with Alan Gray.

"Hello, girls," Alan greeted us. "I guess you didn't expect me, did you?" He plopped onto the couch and stretched his arms along the back. "This is your lucky day. Here's your chance to ask me the things you've been dying to know for years."

Emily, Erica, and I looked at one another. Our expressions were a mix of horror and laughter. "Do you want to interview him?" I offered Emily.

"Oh, that's okay. It's your turn," she replied.

No fair! I thought. *You conduct a two-minute interview with an easy subject, and now I have to interview the idiot of all time.* But she was right. It was my turn.

I sat at the end of the couch, facing Alan.

"Roll 'em," Erica shouted. Pete aimed his camera at us.

"Alan, how was your day?" I began.

"Great. I didn't have to see Kristy, dictator of the universe. How can you stand her?"

I know Kristy can be overbearing. And, from what I'd heard from Abby and Mary Anne, she

93

wasn't being fair to Alan. But she's my friend and I wasn't about to say anything negative about her.

"I don't know what you mean," I replied.

"Yes, you do. You're in the Baby-sitters Club with Darth Vader. You know."

"She's a really effective president," was all I would say.

"You are so full of it, Stacey."

"Excuse me, Alan, but if you're going to be rude to me and insulting to my friends, maybe we'd better not continue."

He grinned obnoxiously at me. "When are you going to get real, McGill?"

"When are *you* going to grow up and stop acting like an immature goofball?"

The taunting grin faded from his face. He scowled down at his hands, which he clenched and unclenched. *Uh-oh*, I thought. *I really hit a nerve.*

Still, I was suspicious and guarded. "What's the matter?" I asked cautiously.

He kept his eyes down as he spoke. "That's what everybody thinks of me," he said. "That I'm an immature goofball."

"Isn't that what you want them to think?"

"Not all the time. Sure, I like a joke. But sometimes I feel locked into that role. No one takes me seriously."

"You're never serious," I reminded him.

"Sometimes I want to be. I try to say or do something serious, but everyone still thinks I'm joking around. To them I *am* a joke. Alan Gray, the human joke."

He was actually being serious. It was hard to believe, but he wasn't kidding.

"Then why do you do things like writing on Claudia's T-shirt when you knew she was planning to use it?" I asked.

He drew in a nervous breath before speaking. "That day I saw Claudia in there by herself and I thought maybe I could talk to her. You know, be friendly. But she just looked up and then went back to her work. *Oh, it's only Alan,* she probably thought. If I played a joke on her, though, she'd think about me for the rest of the day."

"She did," I admitted. "But not fondly."

He shrugged. "That's better than being ignored."

"Have you ever thought about finding some way to relate to people other than by annoying them?"

"I try!" he cried. "I've been completely serious about the film project, but Kristy treats me like I'm a fool incapable of doing anything right."

"That's the only side of you she's ever seen," I said.

"Yeah, but no matter how I act now, she

thinks I'm a clown. How do I change my reputation?"

"I don't know," I replied. "A little bit at a time, I suppose. I see you differently now. Maybe you just started to change your reputation this very minute."

"Cut!" Erica cried. "Excellent."

Facing Alan, I was suddenly uncomfortable. I could be personal in my official role as interviewer. But now, as just me, I felt awkward. "Excuse me," I said and headed for Pete's downstairs bathroom.

I closed the door behind me, then stood and gazed at myself in the mirror. Alan had really surprised me. I realized I needed to have a talk with Kristy. She wasn't being fair to Alan. Was it up to me to tell her?

It seemed there were two uncomfortable conversations in my future. One with Mary Anne. And one with Kristy. I dreaded them.

There was one more thing to be anxious about too. I was the next and last person on our list of interviews. How personal would I let myself be?

How much of the real me did I want to reveal to SMS?

CHAPTER 12

It took me till noon on Sunday to work up the nerve to call Kristy. Yet somehow it seemed easier than talking to Mary Anne.

I picked up the cordless phone and sat at the kitchen table with it. "Hi, it's me, Stacey," I said when Kristy answered. "I have to talk to you about something and I'm not exactly sure how to begin."

"Just say it," she suggested.

"Okay." I told her what Alan had revealed the day before. "He's really trying to change. The things you're doing are frustrating him and hurting his feelings."

"Since when does Alan Gray have feelings?"

"See? I didn't believe he was for real either. But I saw a different side of him."

"Alan is not a person," Kristy replied. "He's a pimple on the face of the earth. If I took him seriously, our film would be as big a joke as he is."

"Come on, Kristy."

"Come on, yourself. Don't you see that he was putting you on? He faked you out."

"Why would he do that?"

"I don't know. To get to me, maybe. He wants to turn our film into an Alan Gray joke and he's using you to persuade me to move aside and let him. Well, I won't."

"I really don't think that's true," I insisted.

"Yeah . . . well . . . I do. 'Bye, Stacey. See you tomorrow." She hung up, leaving me staring at the phone. *She can be the most stubborn person in the universe*, I thought angrily. Of course, I couldn't blame her entirely. She hadn't seen Alan's interview.

As long as the phone was in my hand, I decided I might as well call Mary Anne and get it over with.

"I have some bad news," I began, after we'd said hello. "I mean, it's bad, depending on how you look at it. It's possible to think of it as good news too."

"What is it, Stacey?"

I took a deep breath. "Everyone in my film group thinks your interview is by far the best. They think you came across so well — so much better than everyone else — that they want to keep your part in."

I waited for her reply, but there was only silence. "Are you there?" I asked.

"I'm here," she said quietly. "How about just taking out the part about me being mad at my mother?"

"That's the most interesting part," I answered. "And Emily pointed out that it isn't good journalism to cut compelling material just because it might be upsetting. Not that this is really upsetting. It's just emotional. Don't you think?"

More silence. "Did you even try?" she asked with a quiver in her voice.

"Yes! Of course. I told them how you feel. But, Mary Anne, you don't come across badly. You're a real girl who has a real problem and is talking about it sincerely. Kids will relate to — "

Click.

She'd hung up on me!

Putting the phone down, I let my head fall into my hand. "Well, that went badly," I said aloud to the air.

A glance at the wall clock told me that I was due at Emily's house for my interview in ten minutes. Well, I knew the answer to her first question. How was my day going?

It was terrible.

I wasn't sure how much I wanted to reveal, though. I could get into an even bigger mess if I discussed how stubborn Kristy is and how overly sensitive Mary Anne can be.

No, it would be better to say my day had been fine and keep it light.

Wow! I was thinking just like Emily and Erica. I suddenly understood how they'd felt. I didn't want to sound as boring as they had, though.

Pete had given a meaningful interview without embarrassing himself or creating a mess. I'd try to walk a middle line as he'd done.

When I arrived at Emily's, everyone was waiting in her front yard.

"This will be our last interview before we have to show the film next Friday," Erica reminded us. "We'll use the rest of this week to edit it, and maybe we should film an opening."

"Even though I'm the editor, I'd like to have your help, Pete," Emily said. "After all, you shot the film."

"Sure," Pete agreed. "I'd like to be involved."

Emily looked at Erica and me. "And could the two of you schedule some time to look at the film while we're editing? I've never done this and I could use some help."

"Definitely," Erica agreed.

"No problem," I said.

"Okay, Stacey, this is your moment," Erica said. "Let's go out with a bang." I didn't like the sound of that. "The two of you sit in front of this tree," she instructed us.

We sat. Emily smiled at me. I tried to smile back but I think it came out more like a grimace.

"Roll 'em!" Erica shouted, and Pete turned his camera on Emily and me.

"How was your day today, Stacey?" Emily asked.

"Oh, you know. It's a Sunday. Kind of uneventful," I replied. I tried to control the shake in my voice.

"You seem a little on edge," Emily said.

"I'm not used to being filmed."

"Just relax." Emily asked me a few questions about my life, and I slowly calmed down. I talked a little about my favorite things — math, baby-sitting, fashion. Then she asked how I spend my free time.

"Some weekends I go to Manhattan to see my father and my boyfriend, Ethan," I said.

"Your parents are divorced, aren't they?" Emily asked casually.

Little alarm bells went off in my head.

"Yes," I replied.

"What are your feelings about that?"

Okay, I told myself. *She's just trying to get a good interview. Lots of kids have divorced parents and we haven't touched on that much so far. We need to.*

"It's not easy," I said, trying to select my words carefully and still say what I truly felt.

"At first you think you won't survive. Slowly, though, you adjust. You construct a new world. It's different from your old one, but after awhile you discover that you're okay, despite everything."

"That sounds like a pamphlet on divorce," said Emily.

"Excuse me?" I exclaimed.

"I don't want to be rude, but I don't believe that's how you really feel."

"Are you calling me a liar?"

"Maybe," Emily answered.

"What do you want me to do — start crying? Is that your idea of a successful interview?"

"Do you feel like crying?"

"Well, sometimes," I admitted. "Most kids with divorced parents aren't thrilled about it. Yes, I was glad that there wouldn't be any more fighting. Some nights I lay in bed with my hands over my ears and tears in my eyes just wishing they'd stop screaming. I'm glad that's over. But I'd prefer to live in a happy family with both parents."

"It sounds like you have a lot of anger right under the surface," Emily noted.

"Um . . . well . . ." What did Emily think she was — a psychiatrist? I wished she'd back off. And yet, maybe she was right. Was I angry about the divorce?

I felt cornered. Knowing that the camera

was aimed at me only made it worse. I realized how difficult it must have been for the others.

"It's interesting that your boyfriend lives so far away," Emily continued.

I was glad she was changing the subject.

"Do you think coming from divorce has made you look for distant relationships, ones that don't require too much commitment?"

"I'm committed to Ethan," I replied.

"He lives two hours away," she insisted.

My mouth opened but no sound came out. I was *not* going to fall into her trap and explode. I'd said too much already.

"Cut!" Erica shouted.

"Erica!" Emily protested angrily.

"The tape has run out," she said. From Pete's startled expression I could tell she was lying.

I realized my heart was pounding and my hands were sweating. Erica smiled at me sympathetically. Had she lied to Emily to let me off the hook? It seemed so to me and I felt grateful to her.

Emily turned to me. "I'm sorry if I upset you, but that was a great interview," she said.

I couldn't bring myself to tell her I disagreed. And I didn't appreciate the amateur psychiatry either. "Could we not use the part about my parents screaming?" I asked as my heartbeat slowly returned to normal.

"Are you kidding? That was the strongest part."

A picture of Mary Anne's worried face popped into my head. Now I understood exactly how she felt. And it wasn't good.

Was it too late to undo the damage — for both of us?

CHAPTER 13

Sunday

This wasn't exactly a baby-
sitting job. We filmed Rosie
Wilder while her parents were
there. Rosie, who's a born per-
former, would be a perfect
subject, I thought. It seems,
though, that lately I've thought
a lot of things that weren't so.
Being wrong — what a weird
and annoying experience.

When Kristy told me she'd selected Rosie Wilder for her group's film, I thought it was a stroke of genius.

At seven, she's already appeared on TV several times and in a commercial or two. She's studied piano, ballet, violin, voice, and tap.

From Kristy's point of view, Rosie was sure to deliver something great she could use in the film.

"Do you think we could have a copy of the film?" Mrs. Wilder asked when Kristy, Alan, Anna, and Logan arrived.

"Sure, but she won't be the only one in it," Kristy told her.

"No problem," said Mr. Wilder. "We have a friend who is a film editor. We'll just have all the other children cut out."

"We want to expand Rosie's on-camera portfolio," Mrs. Wilder explained. "That's what casting agents look for, how the child projects on screen."

Rosie came out of the kitchen, twirling a strand of her thick red hair around one finger. "Hi, Kristy," she said. "You want me to be in your movie? That's what Mom told me."

"That's right," Kristy said. "How about telling a joke?"

"Okay," Rosie agreed.

Kristy hurried to ready her camera. She focused on Rosie.

"Knock, knock," Rosie began.

Alan hovered next to Kristy. "A knock-knock joke?" he said.

"Go away. This is great."

"Who's there?" Rosie continued. "Dwayne. Dwayne who? Dwayne the tub — I'm dwowning."

Kristy kept the camera trained on Rosie. The joke wasn't exactly a riot, but Rosie had lots of energy.

As Rosie stared blankly into the lens, Kristy put the camera down. "Rosie, do you know any comedy?"

Rosie looked baffled. "Didn't you think that was funny?"

"It was good but . . . I need something more."

"Show them what you did when you auditioned for the waffle commercial last week," Mr. Wilder suggested.

Rosie frowned. "But I didn't get the part."

"We don't know that yet, honey," her mother said. "These things take time."

"Oh, all right," Rosie relented. "But I need a waffle." Mrs. Wilder hurried into the kitchen and returned with a frozen waffle. She held the waffle up beside Rosie's face. "Go ahead,

Rosie. Say what you said at the audition. Wally's Waffles weally taste gweat!"

"Wally's Waffles really taste great," Rosie repeated without much excitement.

Kristy filmed it. "Not funny," Alan murmured in her ear.

She knew it wasn't funny. "All right, Alan," she whispered angrily. "You tell me when you see something funny and when you want me to film."

Alan threw his arms out wide. "At last!" he cried.

Kristy glared at him.

"I'm sorry that wasn't very good," Rosie said, putting the waffle on a table. "I didn't like Wally's Waffles much so it was hard to say that."

"That's okay," Kristy told her. "I know you take tap. Could you dance for us?"

Alan coughed pointedly, but she ignored him.

"If you really want me to," Rosie agreed. "I'll have to go get my tap shoes." She ran upstairs and clacked back down in her taps. "I need music," she announced.

Suddenly, Rosie's face took on a look of complete horror as she slipped on the wood floor, waving her arms for balance.

"Film! Film!" Alan urgently instructed Kristy.

Without thinking, she obeyed.

Logan leaped across the room and caught Rosie just as she was about to crash to the floor. They landed in a heap in the corner of the room.

Like the football player he is, Logan had even managed to catch a vase as it fell from a table. He sat there with Rosie on his lap and a vase in his hand.

"Rosie!" Mr. Wilder cried as he hurried across the room toward his daughter. Anna followed him.

"Oh, dear," exclaimed Mrs. Wilder.

Rosie's face blossomed into a luminous smile and she turned to Logan. "You saved my life!" she announced dramatically. Then she laid a big kiss on Logan as she wrapped her arms around him.

"Cut," Alan told Kristy.

She put the camera down and grinned at him.

"Now *that* was funny," he said.

Kristy had to agree. Without Alan she might have missed the funniest thing in the film so far.

"Okay, director," Kristy said to Alan. "What do you want to do next?"

"Maybe we can ask Rosie to talk about going on auditions," he suggested. "We might get some funny comments from her."

"All right," Kristy agreed.

Rosie was now standing and feeling fine.

"Rosie, can you tell us about auditioning? What's it like?" Alan asked.

"Some of the people you meet are really weird," she began. "There was a casting agent once who looked like Cruella DeVil." Rosie tossed her head back. She made a face and began to prance across the room. "She looked like this."

"Action," Alan told Kristy. And she turned on the camera.

CHAPTER 14

"Hungry, Stacey?" Mom asked when I returned home that Sunday afternoon.

"Yes, but I need to do something before we eat," I told her.

I took the cordless phone from the kitchen and sat with it on the stairs. I punched in Mary Anne's number and waited.

"Hi, it's Stacey," I said when she picked up.

"Oh . . . hello." Definitely a frosty reception. But I couldn't blame her.

"Listen, I understand why you're mad," I said. "I just came from my interview and now I know how difficult it is. You start to feel trapped and say things that aren't exactly what you mean."

"That's right," Mary Anne agreed. "I don't hate my mother. That's just how I was feeling at that moment. And I only hated her because she wasn't there — because I would love for

111

her to still be alive. But that word *hate* is so ugly and that's all you hear."

"I know. In my interview I made it sound as if I lived in a home with constant screaming. But that isn't true. It was only toward the end, and for just a couple of months. Most of the time I was pretty happy. It didn't come out sounding that way, though."

Mary Anne sighed. "Now it's taped and we're stuck with it, I suppose."

"Maybe not," I disagreed. "I'm going to try again, really hard. I can't promise, but maybe it's not too late to persuade my group to make some cuts."

She wished me good luck and I hung up. I didn't know how I was going to do it, or even *if* I could, but I was determined to try my best.

"Editing is one of the most important aspects of making a film," Ms. Murphy told us on Monday during Short Takes. She stood next to some equipment set up on a table. A control panel about the size of a laptop computer sat next to two VCRs, each with a monitor on top.

"This video editing system is on loan from friends of mine," she continued, patting the machine. "I'm going to tell you how to use it today and then we'll make up a schedule so each group will have time with it."

"What if we like the film we have just the way it is?" Anna asked.

"Very few, if any films are right just as they're filmed," Ms. Murphy replied. "They shouldn't be. It's important to shoot enough material so that you can make some choices about what to keep and what to leave behind. Cutting the film is an art in itself. All your material can't be in your movie. Face it — some of it is probably just plain boring."

I raised my hand and she nodded at me. "What if something in a documentary would embarrass someone? Is it all right to take it out?" I asked.

Emily turned and frowned. I glanced at Erica and Pete. They listened intently for Ms. Murphy's reply.

She folded her arms and gave a small sigh. "That is a very difficult question but an important one," she answered. "I can't give you one simple rule because it's something you have to decide for yourself. Explosive material makes for dynamic, award-winning films. What price are you willing to pay for that? Only you can say."

I wasn't exactly surprised by her answer, but I was a little disappointed. I guess I'd been hoping she'd say people have to come first, or something along those lines. That way I could go to Emily, Erica, and Pete saying, "You heard what Ms. Murphy said." It wasn't going to be that easy, though.

For the next few minutes we watched as Ms. Murphy showed us how to use the equipment. It seemed a little confusing to me, but Pete and Emily would be the ones who were mostly responsible for the editing.

As far as I could tell, you inserted your tape in the first VCR, called the source. Then you marked in the pieces you wanted to use by pressing different buttons on the controller. The controller then sent only the pieces you marked over to the second machine, called the record machine, where they were transferred to a blank tape.

On the controller, there were also buttons marked *audio one* and *audio two*. "These are for sound," Ms. Murphy explained. "Many editors like to keep audio one for dialogue and audio two for music and special sound effects."

"Cool," Pete murmured. I'd never even thought about adding music or anything like that. I wondered if he and Emily had any ideas.

"You can also view your work before making final decisions about what to keep and what to cut by pressing the preview button here," Ms. Murphy explained. "So, as you can see, you have many options when creating your final piece. Another thing I'd like to mention is that

114

if you really don't like a particular scene, you can reshoot it and insert it into your finished film."

We made up a class schedule for using the editing equipment. "It might seem that you have plenty of time, but it will quickly run out," she warned us. "Battles over the use of editing equipment can become very nasty. So use your time efficiently."

Once the instruction ended, Ms. Murphy asked us to break into our groups to discuss how we wanted to work.

We pulled our chairs into a circle.

Our group was next to Kristy's. Before we began talking, I actually heard Kristy say, "Well, what do you think, Alan?"

Amazing!

"I had this great idea," Pete began, pulling my attention back to my own crew. "I was thinking we could use music from the radio that's popular exactly this week. That way we could indicate the time of the video without having to say this is such and such a time."

"I love that," Erica agreed. "Did you understand how to do it on the machine?"

"Yeah. Just make another tape — I could film my radio playing — and mark the music in and out on the audio channel while the visuals are playing."

115

"Sounds good," Emily said. "I was thinking too that we didn't shoot any credits. I could type up an opening with our names."

"Great," I broke in. "Now we need to discuss something else. After my interview, I understood better how Mary Anne felt. Can we please think about cutting her out? It's not as if we don't have enough material. I'd like part of my interview to come out too, but we can leave that in if we take Mary Anne's out."

"No!" Emily cried. "No way."

"Wait a minute," Pete said. "I think I agree with Stacey. We interviewed friends. You guys knew things about the people you interviewed that you wouldn't have known if they had been strangers. So you had an advantage another interviewer wouldn't have had."

"That's true," I agreed. "You knew my parents were divorced. If you didn't, you'd have had to wait for me to reveal that and maybe I never would have."

"You're putting friendship over filmmaking," Emily said stubbornly.

"So what?" I said loudly. (Everyone in the room turned to look at me.) I lowered my voice. "Yes. I suppose that's my decision. To me, friendship is more important than our project."

"Don't you care about the truth?" Emily asked.

"This isn't a film about truth. It's about the feelings of middle school kids. And I care about Mary Anne's feelings."

"Erica is the director," Emily said. "It's her decision. What do you think, Erica?"

A panicked expression came over Erica. She seemed uncomfortable about including Mary Anne's portion of the film against her wishes. Maybe she'd come through for me. After all, she'd helped me out when *my* interview had grown uncomfortable.

"What do you think?" I pressed. "You know how awkward it can make you feel to be taped."

"Do I really have to decide?" she asked unhappily.

"You're the director," Emily pointed out.

"All right," she said. "My decision is . . . Mary Anne stays."

Thumping my desk angrily, I sat back hard in my seat. I felt the impulse to walk out in protest and began to stand up.

Then I sat down again as an inspiration hit me.

There might actually be a way to fix this. I only hoped I could come up with new material interesting enough to make the others want to use it.

CHAPTER 15

"Mary Anne," I said at the end of our BSC meeting that afternoon. We were still in Claudia's bedroom, though everyone but Claudia, Mary Anne, and I had left. "I couldn't convince my group to agree to a cut."

"I don't believe them!" she cried. "Why can't they see that — ?"

I held up my hand to stop her. "I have an idea. Maybe the answer isn't to cut, but to add."

"I don't get it."

I reached into my backpack and took out my mom's camera, which I'd brought from home.

"Oh, no," she protested the moment she saw it. "I'm never appearing on film again as long as I live. Not even at a birthday party."

She began heading for the door. I jumped in front of her. "Listen to me. This can work. We can explain what you really meant."

She stopped and thought. "I don't know."

118

"If you don't like what I film, I won't use it. Just say, 'Off the record,' and I'll burn it or drown it or whatever."

"Give me the camera," she said after a moment. She studied the controls briefly, then turned it on me. "Now, say, 'If Mary Anne doesn't approve of this film, I can't use it,'" she instructed me.

I obliged and she handed the camera back to me. As she sat on Claudia's bed, I aimed the camera at her and turned it on. "Mary Anne, can you tell me how you were feeling the other day when we filmed you?" I asked.

"Yes," she began. "I was having a bad day. I'd had an argument with my stepmother, Sharon, who is a really wonderful person. But even the best person on earth can annoy you sometimes, and . . ."

The interview went on from there.

For the rest of the week, we edited. Pete fell in love with the video editing system. He became obsessed with filming sound, creating audio effects, making visual montages. He and Emily began to get on each other's nerves as they argued over what to do.

Erica and I were less involved. I had to admit, though, that the process was very interesting. "Are you using the new film I submitted?" I asked on Wednesday.

"We're not sure yet," Emily said.

"That's as much a part of the film as the rest of it," I insisted. "It's just on another piece of tape."

"We aren't that far along," Pete told me. "I'll rewind it and you can see it from the beginning."

It looked great. They'd cut the interviews so that only the most dramatic parts were used. And Pete had selected perfect music to introduce each interview.

"Use what I gave you, please," I urged them.

On Thursday, at dismissal, I entered our Short Takes room and found Kristy, Anna, Logan, and Alan viewing their finished film and laughing hysterically. On the monitor, Rosie kissed Logan and announced, "You saved my life!"

"It looks good," I said, smiling.

"Thanks," Logan replied. "I can't wait to show it tomorrow. How's your project coming?"

"I was hoping to sneak a look at it," I admitted.

Kristy shook her head. "Pete was in here finishing up when we walked in. I saw him take the tape out of the machine and leave with it. It looked as if he was just doing some last-minute editing."

I phoned Pete the moment I got home. I had

to know if I could invite Mary Anne to the special premiere of the class movies scheduled for Friday after school.

I kept getting his answering machine, though.

I wondered if he wasn't answering the phone on purpose. Finally, around nine-thirty, his mother picked up and called him to the phone. "Do I need to apologize to Mary Anne?" I asked him directly. "I know you did the final cut."

"I think she'll like it," he answered. "I mean . . . I *think* so. I guess I could be wrong."

"Should I invite her to the premiere?" I asked.

"I wonder if you'll be able to keep her away," he replied.

On Friday after school I waited anxiously outside the auditorium with Claudia. "I told her to come but I don't know if I should have," I fretted as I watched for Mary Anne.

"She was determined to see it for herself," Claudia replied. "It wouldn't have mattered what you said."

Mary Anne showed up just then. She waved but wore an anxious expression. "Stacey, whatever it is, I'll deal with it," she said as she joined us. "The important thing to me is that you tried."

"Thanks," I said. I realized that mattered to me too. I'd taken a stand and let the others know how I felt.

We waited for Abby, Kristy, and Jessi, then walked into the auditorium together. A surprisingly large number of students had turned out for our amateur film festival. Cokie was there with her friends. I'd say close to fifty kids had come, plus at least ten teachers.

A large white screen stood on the stage. Ms. Murphy walked in front of it and gave a quick introduction. Then the films began.

Kristy's group's film was funny. I could barely stop laughing. The next film, directed by Sarah Gerstenkorn, was a funny fairy tale done in Claymation.

Ours was the last. I glanced at Mary Anne. She sat, stone-faced, watching.

Jessi folded her arms anxiously when her piece came on. I wondered if admitting she felt different would make her feel better or worse now that it was out in the open.

Jessi was followed by Abby, who shook her head, as if she were still thinking about it.

"This is wonderful," Claudia whispered to me after her interview ended. Then Mary Anne's face came on the screen. I clenched my fists nervously.

Her interview ran entirely as filmed.

I slumped in my seat. My face came on and my interview ran as filmed too.

But then Mary Anne appeared again.

Thank you, Pete and Emily, I thought.

Mary Anne spoke calmly. Finally she came to her conclusion. "Sometimes you say things in the heat of the moment. You want to take them back. When you're filmed, you can't. The truth is, I love both my mothers. I love the idea of my birth mother that I carry inside me. And I love Sharon."

I glanced at Mary Anne. She was crying, but she was smiling too. She turned and mouthed the words, *Thank you*.

Claudia squeezed my arm. "Good going," she whispered.

Several more interviews ran. Emily had cut hers to about a second. Pete's talk about not wanting to be stuck was very affecting, more than I'd even realized. Cokie and her friends all cheered when she came on.

When Alan came on screen, he let out a humongous burp. The laughter distracted kids from hearing what he was saying on film. Oh well, I guess he couldn't be expected to change completely overnight.

Then I appeared again. I'd turned the camera on myself before handing over the second tape.

"I had a happy childhood before the fighting

started," I said. "The film in my mind recorded lots of happy times. I suppose, in a way, we're all filmmakers, remembering what we loved, editing out what we don't want to remember."

That was the most important thing I'd learned from working on our project. Our memories are little private films. We're all directors, trying to create a picture that balances truth with love and forgiveness.

Dear Reader,

In *Stacey's Movie*, Stacey and her classmates have a chance to make a movie of their own using a video camera. What a great project. When I was Stacey's age, videos and video cameras didn't even exist! I saw my very first movie when I was five years old. My dad took me to the Garden Theater in Princeton, NJ, to see *Swiss Family Robinson*. My ticket cost fifty cents. My dad told me that the first movie he ever saw at the Garden, sixteen years earlier, cost him a nickel.

The year that I saw that first movie was 1960. In 1960, you couldn't go to a store and buy or rent a movie to watch on your television. You had to go to a theater. The first movie I ever saw more than once was *The Sound of Music*. Not long after that, I saw *Mary Poppins* four times — so you can tell how much I liked that movie! As I grew older, I began to watch scarier movies. By the time I was about thirteen, one of my favorite movies was Alfred Hitchcock's *The Birds*. My friend Beth liked it too. We tried to time our sleepovers, which were usually held at Beth's house, for nights when *The Birds* was going to play on TV. Now that I'm an adult, I still love going to the movie theater, but renting a movie to watch at home is a lot of fun too. If I were a student at SMS, I would love Stacey's Short Takes class!

Happy filming!

Ann M Martin

Ann M. Martin

About the Author

ANN MATTHEWS MARTIN was born on August 12, 1955. She grew up in Princeton, NJ, with her parents and her younger sister, Jane.

Although Ann used to be a teacher and then an editor of children's books, she's now a full-time writer. She gets ideas for her books from many different places. Some are based on personal experiences. Others are based on childhood memories and feelings. Many are written about contemporary problems or events.

All of Ann's characters, even the members of the Baby-sitters Club, are made up. (So is Stoneybrook.) But many of her characters are based on real people. Sometimes Ann names her characters after people she knows, other times she chooses names she likes.

In addition to the Baby-sitters Club books, Ann Martin has written many other books for children. Her favorite is *Ten Kids, No Pets* because she loves big families and she loves animals. Her favorite Baby-sitters Club book is *Kristy's Big Day*. (By the way, Kristy is her favorite baby-sitter!)

Ann M. Martin now lives in New York with her cats, Gussie, Woody, and Willy, and her dog, Sadie. Her hobbies are reading, sewing, and needlework — especially making clothes for children.

Notebook Pages

This Baby-sitters Club book belongs to _____.

I am _____ years old and in the _____

grade.

The name of my school is _____.

I got this BSC book from _____.

I started reading it on _____ and

finished reading it on _____.

The place where I read most of this book is _____.

My favorite part was when _____.

If I could change anything in the story, it might be the part when

_____

My favorite character in the Baby-sitters Club is _____.

The BSC member I am most like is _____

because _____.

If I could write a Baby-sitters Club book it would be about ____

_____

#130 Stacey's Movie

In *Stacey's Movie*, Stacey has a great time working with her class-mates on a movie. If I were making a movie, it would be about

_____.

The stars of my movie would be _____

_____

_____. My favorite movie of all time is _____

_____.

The best movie I've seen lately is _____

_____. My

favorite actress is _____. If

I could choose between seeing a movie in a theater and seeing it

on video, I would choose to _____.

STACEY'S

Here I am, age three.

Me with Char
my "alm

A family portrait — me
with my parents.

Johanssen,
sister."

Getting ready for school.

In LUV at Shadow Lake.

Illustrations by Angelo Tillery

Read all the books
about **Stacey**
in the Baby-sitters Club series
by Ann M. Martin

Look for #131

THE FIRE AT MARY ANNE'S HOUSE

As we ate, I tried to ask Sharon about her day at work, but she dodged my questions. She just didn't seem to want to talk about her job. My dad, on the other hand, gave us a blow-by-boring-blow account of this case he was working on, something to do with a property dispute between neighbors. Sharon and I listened politely, but I'm sure if you asked either of us to tell you the details afterward, we wouldn't have been able to.

After dinner, Sharon thanked me and went off to work on her report. Dad headed into the living room to watch a news show, and I went upstairs to call Dawn.

We talked for half an hour or so, about nothing in particular. I told Dawn about the contest the BSC was entering, and she told me about a movie she'd seen. It's always good to catch up with my favorite (and only!) stepsister.

After I hung up, I watched TV with my dad for awhile. Then I headed up to bed, along with Tigger and my book. I read for a few minutes, then turned off the light and went to sleep.

And that was my normal, uneventful Friday. Not a very special day, but one I'll never forget.

Hours later, I woke up. Something was tickling my nose. Tigger! He was walking around on my pillow, making little meowing noises. Sleepily, I glanced at the clock. It was 4:42. In the morning. Why was Tigger waking me up now?

Then I heard it. A regular, high-pitched, shrieking sound. I remembered it from the day, months ago, when my dad had been checking the fire alarms in our house.

Fire alarms?

I sat up in bed.